I Wish My Dog Would Do That!

I Wish My Dog Would Do That!

A Practical Guide to Obedience-training

DAVID KING

faber and faber
LONDON · BOSTON

First published in 1989
by Faber and Faber Limited
3 Queen Square London WC1N 3AU

Photoset by Parker Typesetting Service Leicester
Printed in Great Britain by
Richard Clay Ltd Bungay Suffolk

British Library Cataloguing in Publication Data

King, David
I wish my dog would do that!
1. Pets: Dogs. Training. Manuals
I. Title
636.7′083
ISBN 0-571-15286-4
ISBN 0-571-15287-2 Pbk

Contents

List of Plates

Author's Foreword

On behalf of all dog-lovers I thank you for reading this book because you are clearly interested in creating a good canine citizen. Certainly, with today's ever-increasing anti-dog lobby, dogs need as much good PR as they can get. There is little that can be done about hard-core dog-haters but fortunately these are a very small minority and we can do much to win over the rest. Indeed, I have every sympathy with those who have genuine complaints about the anti-social habits some dogs are allowed to acquire, such as fouling pavements, children's recreation grounds and other public places; roaming free, jumping up with muddy paws, frightening children, worrying sheep and all manner of other unacceptable behaviour. Of course, it is not the animals which are at fault but the owners.

You can help convert the majority of the anti-dog lobby by training your dog to be socially acceptable and persuading other dog-owners to do likewise. Few will disagree that it is our responsibilty to reverse the decline in the popularity of dogs, for the vast majority of them are fine creatures – loyal and faithful, generous and affectionate. The world would be a much poorer place without them. They herd our sheep, guide our blind people, guard our property and possessions, search mountainsides, sniff out explosives and drugs; they help police our streets and perform many other essential tasks. Most important of all is the companionship and comfort they offer countless millions throughout the world.

I decided to write this book especially for the new pet dog-owner and for those who may have had dogs for many years, but who for one reason or another have been unable to train them satisfactorily, or have abandoned the attempt after a number of setbacks. While I deal with complete training from the puppy stage, much of it is equally applicable to adult dogs, although this is a more difficult process. There is a knack in dog-training just as there is in virtually everything and it is much easier than you might think, once you have learnt the tricks of the trade. I hasten to add that I am not implying there is some magical method or unique short cut. There is not, or at least I have never found one.

I have owned dogs of many breeds, shapes and sizes for well over fifty years, and much of what I do with them is pure habit. I should have realized long ago, in view of the remarks constantly being made to me such as 'I wish my dog would do that' or 'I dare not let her off, I would never get her back again' or 'Aren't your dogs well behaved' and so on, that many dog owners just do not have a clue how to set about training their pet. Most dogs can be trained by most owners to a certain degree of proficiency. Few will aspire to Obedience Champion status but the vast majority can become very socially acceptable and a joy to own. Indeed it must be said that some top obedience dogs are trained only in the stylized and precise exercises necessary to win competitions and can be an absolute menace outside the show-ring or training hall. Regrettably others seem quite bemused by the outside world of which they see far too little. Many obedience books have been written, most of which are aimed specifically at this competition sector. My intention is to help the ordinary owner train, and thereby enjoy, his pet dog, but in such a way that all the groundwork is covered should he or she wish to enter the competitive world after the initial training has been mastered. I have set out to provide a simple, progressive training course, resulting in a good canine citizen, acceptable to the owner, and the owner's friends and neighbours, and in consequence a happy and contented animal. I do not disagree with competitive obedience, but I do not believe it should be an end in itself. It certainly was never intended to be so. Dogs should be trained in good all-round obedience first and then progress to the competition ring if that is the owner's wish.

I do not claim that my training method is the only one that can be used. In fact there are many different techniques, but mine is very well tried and tested and I believe it to be the best. Nor can I claim that much of it is original. Like most teachers I have gleaned my knowledge from many sources over the years, tested the many claims and suggestions I have received and either retained or rejected them according to whether or not they worked for me. Some I use and recommend in precisely the form in which I learned them from dog-training clubs, instructors' courses, watching others work, a whole library of books and constant discussions with anyone who will talk with me about doggy matters. Others I have refined or modified to suit my own requirements. What I am offering here is an amalgam of what I consider to be the best practices and advice I have learned, blended with a dash of my own material based upon experience and all the mistakes I have made.

This is probably the appropriate place for me to point out that all the opinions expressed in this book are my own. Others may disagree with me, but I do ask that you keep an open mind on all dog-training matters. This is particularly important should you decide to attend dog-training classes. I thoroughly recommend that you do attend classes because a good instructor can immediately recognize and correct any faults. Also your dog will have the opportunity to socialize with other humans and dogs and this is essential for creating the sort of dog we have in mind. However, instructors are not infallible and some are not even as knowledgeable as they should be. This is why I advise you to keep an open mind. A flexible approach to dog-training is what is required and the conduct of some instructors has caused me to speculate on just how the word 'dogmatic' became part of the English language. Incidentally, a training class is the place for you to learn what and how to teach your dog. It is not a training ground in itself as all training and practice is best carried out quietly at home.

You will obtain the best results from this book if you read it right through initially to get the general idea and then use it as a manual through which to work your way sequentially and at your own pace.

I felt it was important to include a special chapter on 'The Avoidance of Problem Behaviour'. Potential problem behaviour is a subject about which owners should be aware as soon as possible but the solutions pre-suppose a certain knowledge of both dogs and training methods which could not be made available early in the book. The chapter on problem behaviour appears at the end of Part I and I am taking this opportunity of bringing it to the reader's notice. I recommend giving it an early initial reading and then keeping it under review as training progresses.

I would like to thank the Kennel Club for their kind permission to reproduce extracts from their Obedience Test Regulations.

Part I

Basic Training

1

Choosing Your Dog

It is my hope that many of you will be reading this before actually acquiring a dog as I believe I can help you make the right choice. Much of what I say will be quite obvious, but my reason for saying it is to make the potential purchaser think hard before acquiring a dog, thereby avoiding a possibly disastrous impulse buy.

Buying a dog is always something of a lottery, but the risk element can be considerably reduced by exercising care and knowledge. Hopefully you and your dog will be together for a long and happy time. You must realize that once you acquire your dog you accept full responsibility for every aspect of its care and well-being, and incidentally, legal liability as well.

Thus I think the first question one must ask oneself is: Do I really want a dog or is it just a passing fancy? Then: Am I willing and able to look after him? For example, dogs hate to be left alone regularly for long periods. So if you are out all day every day, it would be selfish cruelty to own a dog. You must also be prepared to exercise him regularly and in all weathers and to train him. Don't forget that all dogs need regular grooming and this can be time-consuming with a large, long-haired animal. There is also the question of whether you are prepared to meet the not inconsiderable and ever-increasing annual expenditure on food, veterinary bills, holiday kennelling, inoculations and so on. At the time of writing (1987), I think at least £300 p.a. should be budgeted for the average dog.

My heart sinks whenever I hear a remark like 'I really must buy a puppy for young Johnny'. It is an inescapable fact that dogs and young children just do not mix. Dogs are not toys, not even educational ones, and must not be exposed to the cruelty that can be inflicted on them by youngsters. The time to buy is when and if the child shows respect for and a genuine and hopefully lasting interest in dogs. I could not agree more with the car sticker which says 'Dogs are for life not just for Christmas'. It is a horrifying and disgraceful fact that more than 350,000 unwanted dogs are destroyed in this country alone every year.

WHICH BREED?

Virtually everyone considering the purchase of a dog has some idea of which breed they would like, but before committing yourself, do ensure that it is suited to your circumstances and life-style. A frail elderly lady has no hope of success with a large boisterous boxer, but you do see this combination. After you have selected the breed you feel is right for you, I strongly recommend that you seek the advice of a really knowledgeable person, preferably the vet who will be responsible for your dog after purchase, as to whether that breed is susceptible to any particular problems. For example, some breeds are prone to hereditary blindness, some to hip dysplasia, others to epilepsy and others again to chronic skin problems or respiratory disorders and so on. So my advice is, do your homework to be as sure as possible that you make the right choice.

When you have decided on the breed, further investigation is necessary to locate the best strain for your purpose. There are many bloodlines within a breed, each providing different abilities and characteristics. Quite simply, if you want a family pet, there is little point in paying a considerably higher price for a potential show specimen. Conversely, if you have aspirations in the show ring you are unlikely to enjoy much success unless you purchase from an appropriate show strain. Again, if your requirement is for a working retriever, then it is essential for you to go to a kennel specializing in an acknowledged sporting strain. If I were writing about equines rather than canines I could say it is all a matter of 'horses for courses'. In this all-important matter of selection, there is no short cut. You must attend shows, speak to breeders and especially existing owners and generally acquire as much knowledge of the breed as possible. Books on most popular breeds are readily available from pet shops and book shops and, to a rather less extent these days, from your local library.

WHICH SEX?

Throughout this book I use the word 'dog' in its generic sense, to include both dogs and bitches. It is only in specific instances that I differentiate between the sexes and this is one such case.

Whether you prefer dogs or bitches is largely a matter of personal choice. Bitches tend to be more affectionate, to wander less and be less aggressive, but unless specific action is taken they come into season at six- to nine-month intervals for the whole of their lives. The heat cycle normally lasts about three weeks, at the very peak of which some bitches actively attempt to escape to seek a mate. What is absolutely certain is that any dog picking up the scent will, given the chance, hang around until the heat cycle has ended. A further nuisance is that the bitch leaves blood spots on carpets, furniture and anything else she is allowed to sit on. There are only two ways of preventing a bitch from coming on heat. One is by chemical control, whereby an artificial hormone is administered either in tablet form, or more usually by periodic injections. In my opinion, this course of action is most useful if temporary postponement of heat is required, or if you wish subsequently to breed from your bitch.

I much prefer the second option, spaying, if you require your bitch only as a pet, or when she is no longer required for breeding. Spaying involves the surgical removal of the ovaries and uterus and I am a firm believer in it once a bitch has become completely mature, but not while she is still a puppy. Spaying not only has the tremendous advantage of convenience for the owner, but also gives the animal a definite health advantage. It may well prevent serious illness, and prolong her life. Naturally it also prevents accidental pregnancy and the resulting unwanted puppies. Spaying does not materially change a bitch's personality, but she will probably tend to put on weight if she is not carefully monitored and dieted accordingly, and regularly and sufficiently exercised.

Similarly, dogs may be neutered if this is deemed necessary. They are an embarrassment if oversexed, and castration may also be a cure for aggression in some, but definitely not all cases, depending on the reason for the aggression. Veterinary surgeons are now able to study the effect castration would have on an individual dog before actually committing him to the operation by administering hormone injections over a short period of time.

Experts disagree on the best age for dogs to be neutered. Some believe they should not be castrated until completely mature in order to minimize character change and any tendency to obesity. Other experts, including guide-dog trainers, hold the view that some of the beneficial results may be lost if the operation is not performed before the animal is ten months old. As some breeds mature faster than others, with smaller animals maturing faster than large ones, I recommend that you discuss this matter with your veterinary surgeon in respect of your chosen breed.

In passing, I must mention that my personal choice in veterinary surgeons is for one specializing in small animals rather than one with a mainly agricultural practice. I hasten to add that I have nothing but admiration for that dedicated and very knowledgeable band of men and women comprising the latter group and it is certainly my experience that their charges are considerably more realistic. It is merely that veterinary techniques are so much more sophisticated in this modern age that, as in human medicine, specialization appears to be highly advantageous.

ADULT OR PUPPY?

If you buy an adult dog, you will certainly be confident in the knowledge that he looks just as he should. Additionally, you will avoid the puppy-training phase, although this may prove to be a distinct disadvantage. On the other hand, unless you are familiar with his background and the reason for his changing hands, you will not be aware of his shortcomings. If he is a year or more old it is relatively easy to gauge his temperament, and this can only be advantageous, but if he has spent his earlier life in kennels, he may be difficult to house-train or may show nervousness when confronted with the big world outside.

Adult dogs come from three main sources:

1   From breeding kennels, being either no longer required for breeding, or young adults which were run on for possible retention as breeding stock but subsequently passed over.

2   From previous owners, who for a whole variety of reasons are unable to keep their pets any longer. There are often advertisements for such animals in pet-shop windows, veterinary surgeons' waiting-rooms and the 'Pets for Sale' columns of local newspapers.

3   From an animal shelter, being mainly strays or abandoned animals.

Needless to say, you should try to find out as much as you can about an animal from either of the two last-mentioned sources.

Both heredity and environment influence a dog's ultimate behaviour, with the latter being the stronger factor. With a puppy you can control the environmental factor, but with an adult the personality is already established. By careful selection, you can locate the most suitable strain within the breed of your choice (see p.4), thereby reducing the risk of hereditary faults.

This book deals with the complete training of your dog from the puppy stage, but much of it can be applied equally well to adult dogs, although this is a more difficult task.

MONGREL OR PEDIGREE?

Many people say they would not consider anything other than a mongrel. It is a complete fallacy that only the 'Heinz 57' is the truly hardy, intelligent and desirable type. Certainly one occasionally sees a really attractive mongrel but this tends to be exceptional. All puppies are lovable and cuddly little things but many mongrels grow into most unattractive adults, both physically and temperamentally. Proof of this is the sad fact that the majority of the unwanted dogs which meet a premature end in the vet's surgery are mongrels. If you choose a mongrel puppy you really have very little idea just how he will turn out.

A pedigree dog from a reputable breeder usually makes the best family pet. You know what the breed should be like in terms of size and appearance and what sort of temperament he should have, although, like humans, all dogs are different, even from the same litter, and there are always some bad ones, even in breeds renowned for their good temperament.

The essentials for a pet dog are robust good health and a sound temperament. Good looks are only the third consideration. You should aim for all three, but often breeders place beauty above all else, and although this may win prizes at shows, it is not what pet dogs are all about. However this does mean that you can often acquire an excellent pedigreed family pet at a reasonable price just because he has some superficial flaw in his appearance which makes him undesirable for showing.

There is one other possibility, which is neither mongrel nor pedigree, and that is a cross-bred dog. These are highly desirable animals but are in short supply. Mongrels occur by chance, cross-breeds do not. By cross-breeds I mean deliberate first crosses to achieve a particular result. A good example of this is the crossing of labrador and golden retrievers to produce the ideal guide-dog for the blind. Lurchers result from another deliberate cross – a double cross in fact – which is usually greyhound/border collie bred to pure greyhound. Lurchers are certainly not mongrels and many are very carefully bred indeed over numerous generations to produce the ideal animal for his intended purpose as the supreme hunter. Sometimes whippets are used instead of greyhounds to produce the 'small lurcher'. Many breeders also introduce some Scottish deerhound and even saluki blood to produce the dogs they require.

I must digress here for just a moment to issue a word of caution about the introduction of sheepdog or gundog puppies from truly working parents into the domestic environment. Most of these puppies will have inherited the energy, enthusiasm and a desire to work so strong that they may well be desperately unhappy, and therefore a big problem, if relegated to the role of pet. They could well be happier enduring the hardships all too frequently imposed upon them by some farmers and gamekeepers than the most pampered domestic life. To them the satisfaction of work is an essential of life. If you do consider a dog from this background it must be very well exercised, both physically and mentally, and regularly obedience-trained.

THE FINAL CHOICE

So now you have made all your decisions except one – which dog to select from the litter before you. Please don't be in a hurry at this stage. Personally I like to sit on the floor so that I am on the same level as the puppies. This enables me to observe them more closely and at the same time they do not feel intimidated, as they would if I were towering over them.

Making your choice from a large litter is not easy and time should be taken in the process, not least because I think it is almost as important for your pet to choose you as it is for you to choose him. If a lifetime partnership is to be really success-ful there must be mutual love and respect.

Some people choose the first dog that rushes up to them, but this may or may not be the right dog for your family pet. It may well be the most dominant one – the pack leader type – and not the ideal pet dog. For the ordinary family pet I would not select the puppy which exhibits dominance or aggression towards the rest of the litter. This is the one that will be most difficult to train and handle and the one which will do his best to dominate his owner as well, given the chance. Even more to be avoided is the nervous young puppy which hides away behind his litter-mates or makes off behind the door. He may present a pathetic sight, but you must harden your heart on this occasion. I much prefer the slightly quieter puppy which pauses to weigh me up and then trots over in a friendly and confident fashion, with perhaps a hint of swagger about him.

To summarize, my choice is an animal which is neither excessively bold nor shows any nervous tendency, is intel-ligent and slightly extrovert and, most of all, 'biddable'. By 'biddable' I mean a dog who has the desire to please you. Such a dog usually possesses the submissive instinct, which is a tremendous aid to training, although this must not be confused with nervousness. The ideal dog is submissive without being cowed. Dogs' minds are very complex, some have a very definite sense of humour and they all have their quirks and strange ways. As you go through your lives together you will make many surprising discoveries about your pet – and probably he about you also!

I mentioned intelligence as a desirable trait because personally I like to train an intelligent animal. However, this does not in itself make a dog easier to train as he may often use his intelligence to thwart your requirements. Intelligence is frequently allied to initiative and if biddability is also combined with these traits, you have probably got yourself a first-class dog. Let me give you just two examples.

First, on a number of occasions I have heard experienced shepherds recount how their top-class, certainly very biddable collies have deliberately disobeyed an order, but how later their action had proved correct and the order wrong. As the one on the spot they had the intelligence to realize that the action they had been ordered to take was wrong, so they used their initiative and did what they knew to be right. Similarly, a guide-dog will obey his handler's every command except the one which he knows is wrong and would result in danger. Then he uses his intelligence and initiative to ignore the order and do the right thing.

All dogs must be trained, and very thoroughly trained, but it should be made enjoyable and not so regimented that all initiative is stifled. A good trainer exercises his dog's intelligence, he does not kill it. Some particularly sensitive and intelligent border collies, while they will comply with an order from their beloved boss, will do so with marked reluctance if they see no good reason for that command. It is this type that can be thoroughly ruined and turned into miserable zombies if they are subjected by thoughtless handlers to needlessly long and boring heelwork sessions in which they are hauled endlessly round the training hall.

Finally, your dog must have a good temperament. This simply means he is good-natured with humans and other animals alike. I do not imply that such a dog necessarily rushes up to make friends with every person and dog he sees.

Indeed I think it is most advantageous if he is a little reserved with others but none the less tolerant and completely reliable.

I have already said that the puppy you choose must be brimming with good health, and you can easily obtain a sound idea of his physical condition from your own observations. He must have a lively and alert demeanour, bright eyes and a good coat, and a damp but not runny nose. He should be free from obvious malformations and should move about easily. He should be chubby and well filled-out but not bloated. Inspect his mouth to ensure he has a proper 'bite': his jaw should be neither overshot nor undershot, in other words his upper jaw should not protrude beyond his lower jaw or vice-versa. I think it is well worth asking your vet to examine him thoroughly before you part with your money – one hears so many 'If only I had known' stories.

I have been talking about selecting a puppy from a litter, but most of my advice applies equally well if you are choosing an older dog from an animal shelter or similar place, where sometimes the number of animals from which to select is sadly almost overwhelming, particularly soon after Christmas. Whether you are choosing a puppy from a litter, or an adult from a kennel full of dogs, this is a fairly emotional time and you may well forget to ask the breeder or kennel warden some of the very important things you should know. May I suggest, therefore, that you make a list of all the questions you wish to ask before you go to make your selection.

Two words which must be included in this list are 'worms' and 'vaccination'. All puppies have roundworms and it is essential that they are elimated, both for the dog's health and possibly for the health of all who come into contact with him, especially children. The frequency of puppy worming varies according to personal opinion and the type of preparation used. It is usual for a puppy of eight weeks old to have been wormed at least twice, at four weeks and six weeks. My advice is that you should ascertain from the breeder precisely when your puppy was wormed and the preparation used and then consult your vet about future treatment. I never use a proprietary wormer, always preferring one prescribed by my veterinary surgeon. An adult dog is normally wormed every six months even if he shows no sign of them, although some vets think that an annual worming is sufficient. There are many different types of worms and the preparations used for the periodic worming are formulated to eliminate most of them.

Throughout this book I frequently advise your vet's involvement. Vets are expensive, but it is much cheaper to seek his advice in advance on how to prevent illness rather than wait until a problem arises. Also do not delay visiting his surgery if you suspect something may be wrong. The sooner treatment begins, the greater the chance of success.

All puppies must be inoculated against the four main killer diseases, distemper, parvo virus, virus hepatitis and leptospirosis. These injections are usually given in two doses, at about twelve and sixteen weeks. So your puppy may or may not have been inoculated according to his age at the time of collection from the breeder. If he has, the veterinary surgeon giving the inoculation will have issued a certificate which the breeder should give you. If he has not been inoculated or if only a single dose has been administered you should contact your veterinary surgeon. Also, please remember that annual booster inoculations are essential.

Puppy Education

One of the most frequently asked questions is, 'At what age should I start to train my dog?' The answer quite simply is, 'From the day you take him home.' I like to differentiate between informal and formal training and prefer to call the initial training 'puppy education', with more formal training starting at about six months. The educational training carries on in parallel, because your dog continues to learn, just as we do, every day of his life. It is a sound idea to make a conscious effort to teach him something new, or improve on something he already knows, every day. As with humans, learning capability is far greater in youngsters and declines with the passing years, so you must start your puppy education immediately and make quite sure you proceed along the right lines.

In his natural state, a dog is taught everything he ought to know by his mother. You take the place of that mother and become responsible for him in every way the day he becomes yours. There is a major difference however: you will be teaching him a way of life acceptable to humans, which is quite contrary to his instinctive canine behaviour.

SETTLING IN

Your first responsibility when you take your puppy home is to help him settle in as quickly and with as little trauma as possible. You have whisked him away from the world he knows and from his mother, brothers and sisters, and he has probably been subjected to a car ride into the bargain. No wonder he is lonely, unhappy and confused. He may well puddle, or worse, on the kitchen floor immediately you put him down. Don't scold him and don't frighten him. Just like a human baby, he needs your protection and comfort. Make a great fuss of him and keep him quiet. Don't allow the neighbours to troop in to see him and pick him up and generally handle him at this stage. He just needs you, and this is where you begin to gain the confidence he must have in you all his life. Incidentally, the earlier – within reason – you have a puppy, the more easily and completely he will become acclimatized to humans and the more receptive he will be to subsequent training. Most breeders prefer to keep puppies until they are at least eight weeks old, and in most cases I think this is just about the right age to introduce him to his new home.

The first essential is a good warm bed tucked away in a quiet, draught-free corner, where he will be out of the way. This will rapidly become 'his place', to which he can retire when he wants a little privacy or when you want him out of the way. His bed need not be elaborate and certainly it is inadvisable to buy a nice new basket immediately, as his bed is obviously the most convenient thing for him to chew. The main requirement is that it should be big enough for him to lie in fully stretched when he is a little older and considerably larger. A wooden box (which, if painted, should be with lead-free paint), is quite adequate, or even a large cardboard carton, such as the one your new television set was delivered in. It can easily be replaced if chewed, and with the front cut down to allow access, provides three high, draught-proof sides. Inside there should be a soft and plentiful lining, such as a blanket.

As your puppy is bound to miss the warmth of his brothers and sisters around him while he sleeps, a hot-water bottle inside a secure cover and placed underneath a layer of blanket for the first few nights will do much to make him feel at home and help him sleep.

Unfortunately most dogs cry or howl the first night or two after they are separated from their families. It is absolutely fatal to fall into the trap of going to them, because you will have started a habit which will be extremely difficult to break subsequently. Your dog will know immediately that he has only to cry or howl and you will come running. The only thing to do is to shut the window as a gesture to the neighbours, put your ear-plugs in and go to bed. After a couple of nights it will all be over and you can really get on with the education. Some people advocate getting a very mild sedative from the vet to give to your dog for the first couple of nights. I do not much like the idea, but it may be worth having one handy, just in case the animal becomes excessively disturbed. However, sedation must be discontinued immediately.

As you will readily appreciate, careful, thoughtful and informed education over the first few formative months will make all the difference to the sort of dog you end up with. He has a lot to learn very quickly and environment is enormously important in influencing the end result.

HOUSE TRAINING

This is something with which I have never had a particular problem, possibly because of my mental attitude towards it. I accept that for a while there will be pools and messes at times, particularly at night, because a small young creature just does not have the capacity to hold himself for long periods. So I provide an easily cleaned floor – linoleum or similar – plenty of newspaper and an ever-ready mop and bucket of mild disinfectant.

Most young puppies, if properly encouraged, will become clean in a very short space of time. Older dogs which have been reared in kennels present more of a problem, as do any youngsters who have contracted an illness or disease, such as enteritis, in their breeding kennels. A dog's natural instinct is to be clean, he does not want to foul his nest or the surrounding area. So I blame myself and not the puppy when there is a 'mistake'. If I am too slow getting to him I do not chastise the animal at all, beyond a reasonably mild 'No', and take him outside quickly. The fault is mine because I have failed to read the signs properly and get him outside in advance of the act. You must never rub a puppy's nose in his urine or excreta or even chastise him severely for making a mistake. To do so is extremely cruel. The answer is quite simply to take him outside into the garden at all the crucial times – when he wakes up, after meals, after play, first thing in the morning and last thing at night – and as often as possible in between. One must be constantly on the look-out for signs that he is about to perform. You will soon become familiar with these indications and get him outside fast. You should accompany him and stay with him until he has obliged, otherwise he may well not understand why he is outside in the cold and damp, and just wait to be let in again to make his puddle on the floor. All dogs must be taught from puppyhood to urinate or defecate on command. When you take him outside let him move around freely and then as he is about to squat say CLEAN DOG, or whatever command you choose, and he will very soon get the idea. His strong instinct is to be clean. All you must do is to provide him with the opportunity.

No right-thinking owner will let a young puppy anywhere near a carpeted room at this stage, but accidents do happen and doors do get left open. If he does take a fancy to your best Wilton, thoroughly disinfect the affected area to avoid repetition in the same place.

As I have said, the dog must be taught to defecate on command. It is also of the utmost importance that you decide where you want him to perfom and then ensure he does so in that spot. Ideally this is in the owner's own garden, where the mess can be collected and disposed of. If this is not possible, then a piece of rough ground is the next best thing. However, he should never be allowed to use pavements and other anti-social places. You must be constantly vigilant when you are out with him, and if he looks as if he is about to perform you must say NO and pull him over to the gutter, command CLEAN DOG and let him relieve himself. It is essential that you do not forget to praise him for doing what he was told. Personally I do not like a dog to do his business in the gutter. It is still not far enough away from people, and the dog is himself in considerable danger from traffic. Furthermore it counteracts his training to stay on the pavement. Thus it is infinitely preferable to teach him to use more suitable places before he is taken on to public footpaths, and the gutter should be used only in emergencies.

NATURAL TRAINING

There is a most effective technique which, for the want of a better phrase, I call 'natural training'. Very simply, this is giving the dog a command to do something he is about to do naturally anyway. I illustrated this method when I suggested giving him the command CLEAN DOG immediately you observed he was about to squat. He did squat, thereby obeying your command, and that is a marvellous basis for formal training a little later on. So if he is about to sit, give the SIT command. If he is about to lie down, give the DOWN command and so on. He will then learn these commands and the actions associated with them by the natural method.

At this point I must again stress the golden training rule; always praise your dog for obeying your command. If he is about to sit and you give the SIT command, you must praise him warmly and tell him he is a good dog immediately he sits. In early training you must in fact praise him for even attempting to obey your command, but more of this later.

WORDS OF COMMAND

It follows from the above that as you are going to introduce words of command to your dog at this early stage, you must decide what words you intend to use and stick to them throughout the whole of the animal's life. You must never confuse him by changing your words of command. This is one of the reasons for my suggesting you should read this book right through before you start any actual training. You may then decide precisely what commands you will require, write them down and start training on a sound footing.

I will give just one example of how confusion can result if one word, say DOWN, is used for two different actions. If your puppy gets up on the settee you will correct him by pushing him off and automatically you may say DOWN. Later in training you may give him the command DOWN when you want him to lie on his stomach. The result is confusion in his mind. So you must decide in advance every word of command you will ever use. If you use DOWN when you want him to get off the settee, then use some other command such as FLAT when you want him to lie on his stomach. Alternatively you may use the word OFF when you want him to get off the settee. There are a number of pitfalls concerning words of command and their associated actions. One common confusion arises when a dog is taught the commands SIT and DOWN for the two obvious actions, and then in an unguarded moment the handler instructs him to SIT DOWN. One can see the bewildered look on the dog's face which clearly says, 'What does he want me to do? Sit or lie down?' To help you decide which words of command you wish to use, I have listed all the commands used in this book as an appendix (see p.116).

There are some other words of command and associated actions your puppy must learn at this early stage. The first is his name, which should be used as frequently as possible. A single-syllable name is preferable as even an abbreviation of a long name will confuse him in that he really has two names to learn, his full one and the abbreviation. He will very soon get to know and respond to his name if it is used in a pleasant connection. For example, REX . . . DINNER. When you call him to you, REX . . . COME, and he obeys, make a big fuss of him. You are teaching him two things, his name and to come to you on command. In particular, and this is invaluable in his training, you are teaching him that coming to you is a pleasant experience and therefore an action to be repeated. Start him young and start him right.

BED or BOX is another command he should learn to act upon as a puppy when you want him out of your way or to settle down for a sleep. The command NO is also an absolute must in his early vocabulary. It is used whenever you require him to stop doing something. This is usually something wrong and the amount of feeling you put into the word is dictated by the seriousness of the misdemeanour. It is important that you try to stop him doing something wrong before he does it, rather than while he is doing it; to chastise him after the event is worse than useless. This calls for constant vigilance but is essential. In all dog-training, prevention is better than cure. You must also remember that he does not know something is wrong until you tell him it is. So, as he approaches your new gloves with a gleam in his eye, say NO firmly, and remove the temptation. If there is further persistence on his part, the command must be repeated with considerably more force.

The NO command is negative and while it is a very useful 'catch-all' command it should be used in conjunction with a positive command once your dog has learned other commands. For example, if he is about to jump up at someone, use the command NO to stop him in his tracks and then command DOWN. Later of course when he responds to DOWN immediately, the word NO can be omitted altogether.

LEAVE is another word to be introduced while he is still at the puppy stage, and is used as a preventive command. For example, when you have him on his lead and he pulls towards another dog, you correct him both by pulling him in with the lead and simultaneously commanding him to LEAVE. Later, without the benefit of his lead, he must similarly comply with the LEAVE command.

EXERCISE

It is generally true to say that dogs are given far too much exercise as puppies and not enough as adults. Many well-meaning owners put eight-week-old Sam on his lead as soon as they get him home and drag him out for a walk. Firstly, no animal should be taken outside your own house or garden, or even handled by a stranger for that matter, until two weeks after his second vaccination, as immunity will not have built up until that time. Vaccinations are usually given at about twelve and sixteen weeks. Secondly, puppies do not need any exercise other than that they make for themselves just by rushing around the garden until they are at least four months old, and even older in the case of large breeds, which mature more slowly. It is senseless and harmful to drag a young frightened puppy around on a collar and lead earlier than this.

The early play and exercise sessions in the garden are very useful in furthering a puppy's education. Use his name a lot, get him to come to you, and see if he will retrieve a toy or a ball naturally. Above all this will condition him to look forward to and enjoy his formal training later. Incidentally, don't forget to ensure your garden is dog-proof. Even a large dog can get through a very small hole.

SLEEP AND FEEDING

This is probably an appropriate time to remind new owners that young puppies need a lot of undisturbed sleep. They must not be awakened to be shown off to the neighbours.

They do tend to fall asleep anywhere after a game, and it is a good idea to provide some sort of play-pen around their bed. This confines them to a certain area, even if the door is left open, and also helps you avoid falling over them or stepping on them. Small limbs are very easily broken, and at best you will give your puppy a fright just when you want him to build up as much confidence in you as possible.

It is probably hardly necessary to impress on new owners that their puppy, like a human baby, needs very careful feeding at this crucial time. In any case, breeders will usually provide you with a recommended diet sheet. If you disagree with the diet upon which your puppy has been reared and wish to change it, do so gradually over a two- or three-week period, to avoid upsetting his delicate stomach and generally retarding his progress.

I do not wish to become involved in the subject of feeding in this book but I do most strongly advise new owners to seek their vet's unbiased advice. This will be time well spent and money well saved because avoidable stomach complaints are one of the most common reasons for visits to his surgery.

It is also essential that you train your puppy from the earliest age to allow you to take his food or a bone or indeed anything at all away from him at any time. We all know people who say, 'I wouldn't dare try to take that bone away from him now. He'd bite me!' This is an unforgivable state of affairs, and can be so easily avoided. Small children are often fascinated by dogs feeding and if not carefully watched can easily toddle over and interfere with the animal. Without any doubt the dog will be blamed (possibly to the extent of being put down as dangerous) if he bites, even as a reflex action, but it is the owner's fault, not the dog's, for failing to teach him right from wrong. It is, after all, instinctive for a dog to protect his food. Once you get him used to the fact that if you take his food away he will get it back again, you will have no further problem in this respect. It is all part of the trust-building process.

TRAVEL

Although a young puppy does not need to be taken for walks, you should none the less start introducing him to the big outside world once he has settled into his new home and become acclimatized to you and the family. However, keep him in your arms and do not let other people touch or fondle him until his vaccinations have taken full effect.

In this modern world he needs to know what car travel is all about. Some dogs are naturally car-sick, but others continue to be so throughout their lives simply because they were not acclimatized to car travel as small puppies. Car-sick dogs can be an awful nuisance and it is well worth taking a little trouble to educate your puppy in this respect. To begin with, sit in a stationary car with him in your lap, then let him explore the strange smells around him. Next time, do the same thing but with the engine running. Third time out, let him sit on your lap while someone else drives the car a short distance. As with all dog-training, the 'softly softly' approach is the one which pays off. Most dogs are very quickly car-trained, to the extent that he will probably be in the car as soon as you open the door if you are not careful.

It is an unfortunate fact that a few dogs never overcome car-sickness and there does not appear to be very much that can be done to help these unfortunate cases. One may try using canine travel pills, and in bad cases tranquillizers (prescribed by a vet) can be used to lessen the effect, but I am not in favour of their use on a frequent long-term basis. Incidentally, it is unwise to give a dog either food or water for some hours before making a long journey, but do remember that a dog which has been car-sick is suffering from dehydration and should be offered water immediately the journey is finished.

He must also be trained to be a good passenger and not to jump around from seat to seat, bark and generally be a dangerous nuisance. In a saloon car, he must be taught to sit quietly in the back, if necessary by tying him in with cross-straps. Many modern cars are of the hatchback or estate car type and these are more suitable for the dog-owner. The use of a dog-guard will ensure he stays where he belongs, but personally I like to dispense with this as soon as the dog is trained, and thereafter he must remain in his own place automatically.

It is essential that you do not allow him to jump in and out of the car as he thinks fit. Instead he must be trained, initially on his lead, to enter and leave the car only when so commanded, using the commands Bob ... IN or Bob ... OUT. In potentially dangerous places the use of the lead must be retained at all times.

SOCIALIZING

Socializing your puppy should commence immediately his vaccinations have given him immunity. Socializing is his gradual introduction to other animals and people under all the conditions and in all the places he is likely to encounter them throughout his life. At all costs avoid his being frightened or subjected to any experience likely to undermine his confidence in you. Do not let people maul him about, and do not expose him to intimidation by other dogs. Allow him to get used to his new world gradually and pleasantly.

Most puppies are very apprehensive of road traffic and the effects of a fright in the early months can be permanent. But heavy traffic is a fact of life and he must get used to it. Let him view traffic initially in your arms from a long way back, and gradually move closer over a longish period, until he is happy to sit, with his collar and lead on, in a relaxed manner, quite close to heavy and fast-moving traffic. Don't be in too much of a hurry, and remember that dogs often object to the shock-waves from heavy vehicles more than anything else.

GENERAL GOOD BEHAVIOUR

You must be constantly vigilant to prevent all potentially bad habits from forming. For example, you must immediately stop your dog from jumping up at people. It is marvellous ammunition for a member of the anti-dog brigade to have Bruce jump up and put two great muddy paws on her new white coat. He should be stopped from jumping up before he commits the misdemeanour, but if you are too late he must be pushed down immediately and simultaneously reprimanded with NO, spoken in the sort of voice which lets him know you are not fooling. As a puppy jumps up at you it is often possible, almost as a reflex action, to bring your knee up as he jumps. This has the effect of toppling him over and if used with NO can be a most effective but entirely painless deterrent. I have already commented on the coupling of the NO command with a further positive one once further commands have been taught (see p.20).

Young dogs love to chase things instinctively and through curiosity, just because something moves. If this instinct is left unchecked it can lead to untold future problems and dangers. As we cannot teach other animals not to move, we must teach our dogs not to chase them. The best way is to introduce your dog to all kinds of animals and satisfy his curiosity about them, at the same time chastising him if he makes any attempt to chase them. These introductions should be made very gradually and on the lead. He must first see all these creatures from a distance, and then he may be walked through flocks of sheep and around poultry, etc. He should meet cattle, preferably with a farm-gate between him and them; a young dog is far more likely to be scared by a cow or a bullock than vice-versa. His introduction to cats is not quite so easy unless you have one of your own, but it must be persevered with, by lead-training and the use of the command LEAVE, with reprimands for attempted disobedience.

The only really sound way to stop a dog from chasing is to

25

educate him not to chase anything at all. It is quite difficult to get him to understand that he can chase rabbits but not cats, because there is not much logic in this from his point of view. Both animals are about the same size and furry, so what's the difference? I also believe it is good for discipline if he is stopped from chasing everything. In this connection do remember you are legally liable for everything your dog does, even if you are miles away at the time he decides to misbehave. Thus you should consider the advisability of letting anyone else, and particularly a child, take him out, even when he is fully trained. Incidentally, when I refer to chasing anything, I do mean anything at all. Some dogs show little interest in a live quarry, preferring to test their speed on the paperboy's bicycle or the back tyres of the postman's van. So stop him chasing *anything* and *everything*.

Do not teach your puppy any act, or allow him to do anything which you will later regret. You may think it cute to indulge a two-month-old rottweiler in a game of tug-of-war, but this will not seem so clever when you are trying to wrest something dangerous away from a massive two-year-old who is not prepared to let you have it.

It is natural for all puppies to want to chew things during their teething period, so give him his own *safe* toys to chew. Most puppies soon recognize what is theirs and what is not, and this will do much to preserve your chair-legs, corners of lino and the strap of your best handbag. Rawhide chew-straps are good, but puppies soon learn to demolish them in no time at all. Hard rubber bones are also very useful but they should be checked regularly, as indeed should all puppies' toys, because later in life a dog can use his strong teeth and powerful jaws to chew the ends off the hardest rubber bones and then swallow them. Incidentally I suggest you do not give a puppy objects like old slippers as a plaything, because he will totally fail to understand why you are quite happy for him to chew old slippers into small pieces but get most irate with him for demolishing one of the new slippers young Johnny has just given Dad for Christmas.

However lovable and appealing your puppy or dog may be, please dissuade everyone from either kissing him or allowing him to lick them, particularly on the face. Children, quite understandably, are very prone to this practice, and here it is the human rather than the dog who needs the training.

RECALL

'Recall' simply means getting your dog to return to you immediately, anytime and anywhere. Most dogs wish to be close to their owners – indeed this is the main reason why they come back to you at all. This is instinctive, but for a dog to be properly trained, all desirable natural traits must be augmented by proper and careful training to make them completely reliable. You can effect this by ensuring that returning is a doubly enjoyable sensation for your dog by making a great fuss of him and showing him how pleased you are with him. Some handlers give titbits as a reward, and this may be necessary in some cases, but personally I prefer food as a training aid to be used very sparingly indeed, if at all. This subject, incidentally, causes major differences of opinion between instructors.

The reason why a young dog's natural desire to return to his owner must be strengthened by training is that all too frequently his interest will be stimulated by something or someone else – a child playing with a ball, an interesting smell, another dog. The list of potential distractions is endless. So he must be trained to return to you as a reflex action, a command that he never considers disobeying.

In the very early days of training it seems inevitable that the youngster will choose the most public place possible to disregard his Recall, and we have all seen the farce which follows, if the owner is not careful. The owner calls. The dog remains oblivious. The owner calls again and again, each time more loudly and with a growing edge on his voice. The dog continues to ignore the Recall, so the owner walks towards him, and as he does so the dog moves further away, just out of reach. The owner moves forward faster, the dog back-pedals even faster. Few owners are quicker and more agile than their young dogs, and anyway Fido is beginning to enjoy this chasing game almost as much as the spectators. Eventually he gets tired, gives up and returns to his now very frustrated and irate owner, and more often than not is subjected to a good spanking. The owner may feel a little better after that, and having put Fido on his lead proceeds to drag him home. One thing can be predicted with complete certainty: next time Fido will make sure he is not caught. The owner has completely mishandled the situation and made at least three major mistakes, which are well worth analysing here.

1   The owner chased his dog, thereby creating a precedent for all time. The golden rule is *Never move towards your dog . . . Make him move towards you.* I can hear you comment, 'That is easy to say but difficult to do.' That may be so, but patience is essential in all dog-training matters and never more so than at this critical stage. All young dogs will return to you ultimately, but must be encouraged to do so. For example, a dog will usually chase after you if you turn around and run off in the opposite direction, or run backwards as fast as you can, calling his name in an excited fashion. This is another good game for him, but the difference is that he is playing your game, not you his.

2   The owner lost control and let the dog provoke him into changing his tone of voice. Your voice is your most important training aid. Any dog is discouraged from returning should a hostile reception be a probability, so maintaining a pleasant and welcoming tone of voice is essential.

3   The owner's greatest mistake of all was thrashing Fido when he did return belatedly. This will have set back his

training significantly, and in the case of a very sensitive dog it may have ruined him for all time. Prior to this the dog had been rapidly building up his trust and confidence in his owner. Now he has been hit and his trust has been severely dented if not totally shattered, and he is confused into the bargain. Every other time he returned his owner made a great fuss of him and told him what a clever dog he was, but not this time. His world is shattered. So even if it takes you half an hour to get him back and even if you have missed your favourite television programme, it is essential that you praise him and welcome him back, as they say in the dog-training world, 'even through clenched teeth'. Dog-training is not easy but it is certainly full of interest!

There is another way in which you can quite unwittingly discourage your dog from returning to you when he is thoroughly enjoying a good romp on the common or in some other wide open space. You decide it is time to go home, so you call him and he comes to you with all the pleasure and enthusiasm he has demonstrated in the garden. This time his reward is to be captured, put on his lead and dragged off home. Small wonder he soon learns to keep his distance when he thinks playtime is over. So make a game of this as well. Call him to you, make a fuss of him as you put on his lead, walk a few paces then release him again. Do this a number of times and when it really is time to go home, again make a big fuss of him, give him a titbit and generally make him feel life is not too bad. Improve the situation still further by giving him another titbit when you get home.

COLLAR AND LEAD

Quite early in your dog's education you will be introducing him to his collar and lead. The best collar is a lightweight flat leather one. Put it on him quietly when he has had a romp and is in a relaxed frame of mind. Some dogs take very little notice beyond a few shakes of the head or a couple of indolent scratches at the collar. A few behave rather like a bucking bronco which has just been saddled for the first time. When he accepts the fact that he has to wear his collar, tell him with a lot of sincerity in your voice what a good lad he is and take the collar off. Repeat the following day but for a longer period. After a day or two, wearing the collar will be taken for granted, so now a lead can be attached.

Provided it is a light lead, let the dog trail it around behind him for a short while. He is probably curious and hopefully will choose to investigate it rather than rebel against it. Now pick up the lead and stand still. If he remains quiet, all well and good, but if he starts to pull away and struggle to free himself from the lead, remain quite still and do nothing, and sooner or later he will give up. When he does so, coax him to come towards you. Do not tug his lead but say HEEL in a very warm, friendly voice and pat your thigh. If necessary squat down to his level. It may take some time and not a little persuasion, but he will come in the end, and then you should make a great big fuss of him.

Now move forward a couple of paces and again coax him to follow you by voice, patting your thigh and putting the very lightest pressure on the lead. He will soon get the idea of walking with you and indeed there should be little problem if, like most puppies, he is used to following you around quite naturally when off lead.

So much for the puppy who is reluctant to follow you. However, the opposite problem frequently applies, particularly with a keen young dog, whereby he will pull strongly and attempt to tow you along behind him. This is not a fault which will disappear of its own accord or in the fullness of time. If not corrected immediately he will pull with increasing strength for evermore, and every walk will be sheer misery for you both. To correct him let him pull away from you and then jerk him back, giving him the firm command HEEL. This can be reasonably gentle at first, but as he pulls away again jerk him back harder and issue the same command but in a much firmer voice. Hopefully he will soon get the idea that it is much more comfortable for him to walk quietly on a slack lead than to try to pull you along. As always, praise him warmly once he makes a genuine attempt to comply with your command. This will reinforce his greater comfort with the knowledge that he has done something to please you.

A puppy will usually quite quickly give up his attempts to tow you along, but an adult dog which has had the bad habit for a long while will probably need greater correction and the application of much more force. If the pulling fault cannot be cured with the ordinary flat leather collar, you must resort to the use of a slip-chain, or a check-chain as it is sometimes called. I do not hesitate to put this on a hard-pulling adult, but I do not normally favour using it on a puppy under five or six months old, although it may be necessary to introduce it earlier in difficult cases. This part of the training may seem rather harsh and it does cause the animal considerable discomfort, but it is far less cruel to get it right now than have him half-strangle himself every time he goes out for the rest of his life. Remember, however, when correcting him that you should use only the minimum force necessary to achieve results and that all attempts to obey you must be profusely and immediately praised. In all training there should be much more praise than correction. It must be fun for you both, not just hard work.

There are a number of different designs of slip-chain but for general purposes the most common type, the single slip-chain, is quite adequate. All too frequently this is referred to as a choke-chain, or choker, and that is just what it becomes if it is used incorrectly. To avoid such cruelty you must ensure you have put it on correctly each time you use it. Even when used correctly it causes the dog a certain amount of pain, but of course the whole idea is to make him comply with your command, and once he does so, the chain is released and the discomfort ceases immediately. The remedy rests with him. I have already mentioned that only the minimum amount of force should be used to effect compliance, but this varies very considerably according to the type of dog. A small woman may well find it difficult to muster enough strength to correct a strong and wilful young adult German shepherd dog (Alsatian) with his powerful and well-covered neck, whereas a fraction of that power applied to a whippet with his delicate neck and velvety skin, would cause him great agony and could well spoil him for ever. It would be sheer cruelty. Indeed, it is infinitely preferable to use the double slip-chain design on such an animal.

The single-slip collar is a length of chain with a ring at each end. To make it into a collar, hold one ring between the thumb and forefinger of the left hand and the other ring with the right hand, and then allow the chain to pass through the ring in your left hand (see pl.1). The lead is attached to the ring previously held in your right hand. With the dog standing or sitting on your left, facing the same way as yourself, and with the ring to which the lead is attached in your right hand, pass the collar over the dog's head (see pl. 2). This means that the ring through which the chain passes comes beneath the dog's neck. The collar tightens when it is pulled, but slackens immediately it is released, by means of its own weight. However, if the collar is put on upside down it will tighten but will fail to release when slackened, thus maintaining the 'choke' effect, which is both cruel and worse than useless. To be fully effective, the slip-chain must be the right length, just long enough to pass comfortably over the dog's head.

The slip-chain should be used for training only. It is not a substitute for a leather collar, and can be lethal if the dog is allowed to run loose wearing it. Similarly, he should not be chained up by his slip-collar, although this is seen all too frequently.

When your puppy is thoroughly happy with his flat collar and lead and when he has got used to traffic and knows the

SIT and HEEL commands, he should be taught road-crossing. He should be stopped at the edge of the kerb every time, whether or not there is any traffic about, and made to sit quietly. He should then be commanded to HEEL and walk calmly across the road at your side. The puppy will very quickly learn his kerb-drill providing you exercise proper self-discipline and stop at the kerb every time, not only when you have the time or feel like it. If you want your dog to be wholly reliable, you must be consistent yourself.

Indeed, your whole family must be totally consistent and self-disciplined in the dog's upbringing and training. One member of the family must not be allowed to encourage him to do something which someone else totally forbids. The result will be a confused and unhappy dog. Therefore it is a good idea to have a family meeting, before you bring your puppy home if possible, to thrash out every matter pertinent to his upbringing and lay down a comprehensive set of responsibilities and hard-and-fast rules to which all must adhere.

It is well worth spending as much time and effort as possible on your puppy's education. It must be self-evident that sound and correct groundwork at this most impressionable time is essential if he is to turn out as you intend.

3

Training Theory

I believe there are two distinct aspects to the theory of dog-training. First, it is necessary to understand something of the workings of the canine mind to see how the handler can apply this knowledge to practical training. Second, one has to consider the attitude the handler must adopt for best results. From now on it seems more appropriate to use the word 'handler' rather than 'owner', although in most cases these are synonymous.

THE CANINE MIND

Today's domesticated dogs were evolved over many thousands of years from the original wild dogs and are particularly closely related to the wolf. They were selectively bred for the sole benefit of mankind. Their useful traits and instincts were developed and the undesirable ones suppressed, to enable dogs to live in close proximity to man. Specialized talents were developed, such as the instinct to hunt by scent or by sight, to guard, to herd, to haul loads and so on. One has only to consider today's wonderful guide-dogs for the blind to realize how sophisticated selective breeding programmes, coupled with specialist training, have become. Border collies are selectively bred for their intelligence, stamina and an ability to work on their own initiative. There are few better spectacles than a collie working sheep high up a mountainside.

Thus today we have many fine breeds which are completely diverse in their size, appearance, capabilities and talents, because that is how they were developed. All have the basic canine instincts, but the remaining traits have been accentuated or suppressed according to man's specific requirements. Therefore when we select a pet dog we must be aware of his hereditary strengths and weaknesses and start our obedience-training accordingly.

As I said earlier, most breeds can be obedience-trained to a greater or less extent. The breeds most usually seen at obedience shows are the border collie and the German shepherd dog (Alsatian), but many other breeds are highly trainable. Most working and guarding dogs are very suitable for obedience, including the bearded collie, sheltie, doberman and rottweiler, as are many gundogs, especially the golden retriever, labrador and some spaniels. The list is relatively long, with other breeds such as the poodle (especially the standard poodle), boxer, Belgian shepherd dog and corgi immediately springing to mind.

Let us now look a little closer at what lies inside the dog's mind. Firstly we must understand that in his natural state all his actions result from the instincts to which I have already referred. If he is hungry, he will look for food, and if that food is our unguarded Sunday joint, then that is what he will take. It is no good expecting him to have human ethics. He has not the slightest idea he is doing wrong until we teach him otherwise.

If he transgresses any rules of canine behaviour while he is a puppy still with the litter, his mother will chastise him, usually with a warning growl. If he persists, the reprimand will be immediate and severe, and will normally involve the dam shaking him by the scruff. This in itself is instinctive to the dam, and also very effective.

Thus every dog has an instinct which we call stealing, but it is not an action for which he would be reprimanded by his mother because it is not contrary to the rules of canine behaviour. However, as this instinct is not acceptable in human society we must suppress it. This is achieved firstly by education and training; then, when he understands he must not help himself to the Sunday joint, he must be immediately and severely reprimanded if he tries to do so, because he now knows he has done wrong.

On the other hand, in the chapter on puppy education I referred to the dog's instinct to be clean and not foul his nest (see p.17). This is a desirable instinct for the human environment, so we encourage it.

This brings us to an absolutely crucial rule of training. The dog must be taught precisely what he may or may not do, but never reprimanded for a misdemeanour until it is absolutely clear that he understands. He must always be given the benefit of the doubt. It is worse than useless to punish a dog if he does not know the reason for it. You are bringing him up in a world completely foreign to his natural instincts, so you must painstakingly teach him all the new rules you are imposing, one by one. All too frequently one sees dogs being cruelly chastised for doing something the owner, in his ignorance or stupidity, thinks the poor animal should know without being taught.

Some learned people insist that dogs have no power of constructive thought, no gift of logic. While this may be true of some breeds I do not think it is universally applicable. I am sure many intelligent animals from certain breeds possess a basic form of logic which is a great aid to their learning process. Certainly, all dogs, whether blessed with logic or not, learn by experience and repetition. The variable factor is the time it takes them to learn a particular thing. Fortunately they have very retentive memories, so a lesson once thoroughly learned is not easily forgotten.

The dog's mind is such that if he does something and it is a pleasant experience he is happy to do it again, but if it is unpleasant he will refrain. If he repeats an action with unpleasant result a few times, his memory (that is, his experience) will very quickly register the fact that that action is to be avoided in future. Thus a handler uses a training technique called 'correction and reward'. It works like this.

If a dog does something of which we approve he is rewarded. This is pleasant and he is happy to repeat it. If he does something unacceptable to us he is corrected. This is unpleasant so he will refrain in future. In actual fact correction is applied in two ways. First, we must correct errors in training caused by lack of understanding. This is usually done by ignoring the error, neither scolding nor praising, but repeating the exercise, making sure he gets it right next time, in which case he can be rewarded. The other use of correction is reprimand or punishment for deliberate disobedience (making absolutely sure the act was deliberate and not the result of lack of understanding). Such correction can be vocal or physical or both. The dog is scolded mildly or severely according to the severity of the misdemeanour. A suitable correction for a serious offence is to shake the dog by the scruff just as his mother would have done.

A moderately severe but most effective verbal correction is the word BAD (or BAD DOG) spoken in a most uncompromising voice. (Incidentally the voice need not be loud to be effective. Use only the minimum volume necessary as dogs have very acute hearing. It is the tone of voice which is all-important.)

There should be much more teaching and praising and mild correction than severe correction. Mild correction is used for such offences as momentary loss of concentration, with severe correction being reserved for wilful disobedience or sheer naughtiness.

It is vital that the handler should be aware of just how hard or soft his dog is, just how dominant or submissive, brash or timid. A mild vocal reprimand to a sensitive animal may be more devastating than a severe shaking is to a dominant dog. I do not normally recommend hitting a dog, or even making threatening gestures at him. Striking any dog other than a very dominant one will be over-correcting; this will result in a severe loss of his confidence in you, and as I have already said there must be mutual love and respect for the canine–human partnership to work satisfactorily. If you hit or threaten a very dominant animal, particularly if he is large and powerful, he may well decide to fight it out there and then, and probably come off best. I have known this to happen with the most tragic consequences, which is precisely why I advised anyone buying a dog as a family pet not to select the most dominant in the litter. In the canine world there is a top dog and a bottom dog (a bit like the human race, now I come to think of it!). There is a pecking order and the top dog is the pack leader. All the rest are subservient to him, and then to number two dog, right the way down to the poor bottom dog, to whom every other dog is superior. We all know that a canine pack leader will fight to maintain his position, and with a really aggressive dog it matters little whether his opponent is another dog or a human. Incidentally, never be tempted to smack your dog's nose. It may seem a very easy and convenient target for you, but to the dog it is a particularly valuable and sensitive organ and easily damaged.

This conveniently brings us to the next major keystone in our relationship with our dog. We must be his pack leader, the Boss, and it is a curious fact that most dogs will readily allow a human being to assume this position. It is because of this that they give us respect, and are prepared to obey us, in most cases quite willingly. If, on the other hand, we are unable to dominate him, for whatever reason, and to become his pack leader, we shall gain neither his respect nor his confidence and the process of correction and reward will just not work. Any animal which will not accept his handler as pack leader is not suitable as a family pet.

So much for correction, now for reward. Reward is usually by voice, praising your dog and telling him just what a good boy he is and how clever he is and so on. He doesn't understand the words, but he understands the tone of voice and he knows he has done right . All dogs like to please those they

38

respect, and their reward is complete when they are praised for it – a very pleasant sensation for him and therefore one to be repeated. Occasionally reward may extend to a titbit, but I have already expressed my opinion on the general use of food as a training aid.

The mind of an intelligent dog is so acute that some people believe dogs possess an additional sense or extra-sensory perception, that they can read our minds and so on. A very few dogs particularly in tune with their handlers may conceivably have some sort of telepathic communication but generally I believe the explanation is rather more mundane. What the dog does have is extraordinary perception. He observes the slightest movement we make, every change in tone of voice, and so on, and these are filed away in his memory for subsequent immediate recall. Over a period of time he learns every aspect of our daily routine, and so appears to know what wᵒ are going to do before we realize it ourselves. The trigger by which he knows that he is about to go out for his last walk is far more subtle than the end of the ten o'clock news, or your picking up his lead. He may go for his last walk any time between ten-thirty p.m. and midnight, but he does not make a mistake and get up from his snooze at the wrong time. Instead, by some minute action we unintentionally signal to him that it is time to go out.

This acute perception is of immense help to us when training. In time an intelligent animal will respond to the smallest signal. The twitch of an eyebrow is sufficient. For example, most dogs will soon learn that if you step off with your left foot, as in heelwork, he is to accompany you, but if you step off with your right foot, as in the Stay exercises (see pp.67–71), he is to remain. This is command enough without any other order, either vocal or by hand-signal.

One frequently hears people attempting to train their dogs as if they should automatically understand English, their tone of voice getting higher and higher as frustration mounts because the dog does not react to the commands. It must be remembered that a dog has to learn the sounds (the words) and the associated actions just as we do. We have already seen the extraordinary perception most dogs possess, so all we have to do is to instruct him in all the sounds we will use for commands and the actions he is expected to perform in response, one by one.

Before passing on to the next subject I would like to leave you with this thought: *an obedient dog is a happy dog*. He is happy because he knows his place in human society. He knows what is expected of him. He is not chastised for some reason he does not understand. He is accepted and made a fuss of. He is taken to places where a badly behaved dog would never be allowed. He is loved and respected by his handler and has the joy of reciprocating that love and respect. So much for Rex, now let us have a look at our side of the bargain.

THE HANDLER'S APPROACH

Firstly we must consider the training aids available.

SLIP-CHAIN (OR CHECK-CHAIN) AND LEAD

We have already dealt with the slip-chain and its use (see p.31). The length of the lead to which the chain is attached will obviously vary with the height of the dog but 3½ – 4 feet is the average length. There should be just enough slack in the lead when held in the right hand at stomach level to allow the handler to tighten the slip-chain with a minimal movement of the right hand – little more than a flick of the wrist.

Incidentally many of the 'loops' sold as substitutes for slip-chains are made of materials other than metal and some of them do not loosen when released. The whole idea of the slip-chain is that it can be both tightened and released instantly. Any device which does not operate in this way is both cruel and ineffective. It is a strangling device, not a training aid.

HANDS

Hands are used in three ways. First, they are the connection between you and the lead, and as such should be used with a sensitivity rather similar to that needed on the reins of a horse. You can convey your every mood to your dog via the lead. Second, hands are used to give signals to your dog. It is strongly recommended that during training you command your dog both by voice and by hand signals. This gives him the best possible chance of learning and ultimately he will be able to work on either one or the other. Third, you use your hands either to direct the dog into the right position or physically to place him correctly in such exercises as the Sit. However, as a general rule dogs should be touched as little as possible during training, but encouraged to do it all for themselves.

VOICE

I have already commented on the use of the voice so I will just summarize here by saying that not only is it the most important training aid of all but also the only means of control once the lead has been removed. Properly used, it conveys everything from pleasure and praise to the most severe correction.

The remainder of this chapter deals with more of the essential rules for successful dog-training. They are vital and should be carefully studied and completely understood. I suggest you refer to them frequently during training to check that you are doing everything correctly. If during training you encounter any difficulties or problems, you may well find the solution by re-studying these 'do's and don'ts'.

1 Do not hurry your training. If you are short of time, postpone the session until you can give it the necessary attention. Do not be impatient to pass on to the next lesson. While more than one thing may be taught at a time, keep progress to

a level both you and your dog find comfortable, and keep on returning to lessons previously learned with the object of polishing each one to a degree as near perfection as possible. Repetition with improvement is the key to success. Dogs need mental stimulation as much as physical exercise to keep them fit and happy and their daily obedience session does much to keep their minds active.

Progress often seems very slow to the handler. Don't despair, and remember, you see your dog every day. His advancement will be quite obvious to someone who sees him at less frequent intervals.

All training must be carried out on the 'building-block' principle, a new exercise being based on the experience of the ones already learned. The more complex exercises are broken up into their various logical parts and each part taught separately. It is only when all the components have been thoroughly mastered that the whole exercise is put together. It also allows you to re-train or polish any element individually without interfering with the other parts of the exercise.

The length of time you spend on your daily training will depend mainly on the stage you have reached. I am referring to formal training because 'education' is a continuous process. Initially, five minutes two or three times a day is ideal because a young dog easily gets bored and to continue would be counter-productive. The length of the session is increased as more exercises are learned and you must be the best judge of what is ideal for you and your dog, but always break off before boredom sets in. Normally I find a fifteen- or twenty-minute session quite sufficient, sometimes once and sometimes twice per day. Occasionally our sessions are considerably longer when we get a bit carried away with what we are doing. For an older dog who has mastered many exercises, a five- or ten-minute session just to keep his hand in is probably enough, revising different exercises each day on a cycle basis.

2   You must concentrate on your dog, just as you require him to concentrate on you, and progress is only possible if you give him your undivided attention. You will probably find this extremely tiring. You are virtually willing him to do it correctly, and this uses a lot of mental energy – another reason why sessions must be short. Skip the session altogether if you are feeling tired or disgruntled. It will only harm you, your dog, and your mutual relationship if you press on under such circumstances. If you feel your temper beginning to slip during a training session, stop immediately, have a little game with the dog and finish on a happy note. This way, he will look forward to his next training session. All training must be fun and enjoyable for you both. Don't make it a chore.

A training session does not mean continuous training. Do one exercise, have a short break for a romp or a game with his favourite toy, and then do the next exercise, but concentration must be absolute for you both when you are actually engaged in the exercise. Therefore let your dog know precisely when he is working and when he is not. He will soon get the idea if, for example, you use the word FREE when he is released from an exercise, and in the best shepherding tradition THAT'LL DO when the session is over.

Where a dog is more advanced in his training, it is advisable for him not only to have a short break to relax between exercises or individual elements of more complex exercises, but also to do a little heelwork for just a minute or so. This will help him clear his mind of the previous exercise and avoid possible confusion. There are, in fact, certain conflicting exercises which must not be taught or practised in the same session. These will be discussed in detail as they arise. Also, as the dog begins to build up a repertoire of exercises, vary the sequence in which you practise them, otherwise he will anticipate and not so much act on command as perform a routine rather similar to a circus act. Incidentally you should never wear loose clothing or have straps or cords dangling whilst training, as this tends to break a dog's concentration.

3 Try to prevent your dog making a mistake. This is easy to
say and difficult to do, but it must be your constant aim. You
can of course correct a mistake, but it is much easier if the
error is avoided in the first place. If you are really concen-
trating on your dog and ensuring that his attention on you
never wavers, you are going a long way towards avoiding
mistakes. With time and experience you will learn what
potential mistakes are about to happen and prevent them
before they occur.

4 You must have *complete control* over your dog at all times –
not only when training. Complete control means both complete obedience and immediate response. This must be insis-
ted on every time. He must never be allowed to get away with
disobedience, not even once, because that is the thin edge of
the wedge. This can be very hard work sometimes, but you
will gain proper response from your dog only by never giving
in to him. You are the Boss all the time. In training, make sure
your dog complies with a command by using slip-chain and
lead, voice and hand-signals where possible. When he has
learned a particular exercise he must always comply with that
command immediately, but you must never give him a command he does not understand. You must show sympathy and
patience but you must also proceed with quiet determination
to ensure that he always obeys your order.

Remember that at the outset our aim was to produce a truly
socially acceptable dog and his behaviour when he reaches
adult status reflects on you and the standards you are prepared to accept. Therefore always insist on the best he can
give you.

5 All dogs are different and you must get to know your pet
completely before you can train him efficiently. Dogs are not
unlike children and we all know that the method for teaching
each child should be tailored to that child's individual nature
and capabilities. We must know how much each child can
absorb and how quickly, and we must know whether the

'carrot' or 'stick' approach is the more appropriate. It is just the same with the complex canine mind. Once you know your own dog totally, you can shape your training techniques accordingly.

6   Be absolutely certain within your own mind precisely what you want from your dog before you start training. Plan ahead, decide on the words of command you propose to use and then be consistent in the commands you use, your method of teaching and what you teach.

7   I have already dealt in considerable detail with Correction and Reward. This is of course the basis of our training technique, so do remember that you must never chastise the dog for doing something wrong unless you are 100 per cent sure he fully understands the command, and then punishment must be immediate. He must always be given the benefit of the doubt, but must still comply with that command albeit under instruction. However he must always be praised for success or even for the attempt. Reward by praise must be profuse at the beginning but harder to earn as he gets older and more proficient. He must work for his rewards, otherwise they are valueless. Remember also that the change from correction (harsh tone) to reward (praise, friendly tone) is immediate, and then back again to correction (harsh tone) immediately if necessary. You must have virtually two voices and the ability to switch from one to the other instantly.

Your dog's respect for you will increase if your correction for disobedience is based on fair-mindedness but you will achieve the reverse effect if you nag him either by voice or such niggling acts as repeatedly tweaking his slip-chain. Do not threaten him with what you will do if he doesn't improve in the future; this is meaningless and destructive. Your correction should be immediate and as severe as the misdemeanour requires; it should then be forgotten. Nagging also includes the constant repetition of commands. Once is enough. Dogs have a definite sense of dignity and need to be treated with respect. They do not like to be made to appear ridiculous and this should be avoided even when they are being chastised. Most dogs are quite prepared to have some fun with you and to amuse you but this is deliberate. They may be laughed with but not at.

8   Try to vary your training locations and the times of day you train because you want your dog to be obedient anywhere and everywhere at all times.

9   Only one person should carry out the formal training but other members of the household may take him out and the dog should obey them as he does his handler.

10   If you have more than one dog, never train them together. If possible don't even train them within sight or sound of each other. The concentration of the one being trained will be broken and the other will become thoroughly frustrated at not being part of the action. They really do enjoy their training if you approach it correctly, and resent being left out.

11   Always be on the look-out for potential nasty traits or bad habits and stamp them out before they begin. The old adage about prevention being better than cure still applies.

12   In the chapters which follow I shall be describing specific exercises in detail, and in certain cases I shall suggest alternative methods of teaching. I have already pointed out that there are many teaching techniques and while those I recommend are well tried and tested they are certainly not the only ones. Every animal finds some exercises difficult and others easy, and what is simple to one may present great problems to another. Therefore don't persist too long with any exercise which is proving particularly difficult to teach. Instead, try to analyse why your dog is having problems and just what is causing the mental block. Then try it another way. Often the solution is very simple, and there is every advantage in your

innovating, improvising and experimenting. No one has all the answers, but often it helps to talk to other handlers, or instructors at dog-training classes, to see what ideas they have. Then go home and try them all out and see which suggested method gives the best result. Don't be hidebound, find out the best way for you and your dog.

Having finished this rather long but vitally important catalogue of do's and don'ts, let us now proceed with the formal training exercises. If we are to achieve our aims these exercises are necessary for all pet dogs, but I have presented them in a form suitable for the Beginner and Novice Classes of official obedience competitions should you wish to progress in that direction at a later date.

I have referred to the Kennel Club Regulations for tests for Obedience Classes at various places throughout this book. These are current at the time of writing, but as they are apt to be revised quite regularly you are advised to check them if you wish to enter competitive obedience. The easiest way to do this is via your local dog-training club, or you can purchase the *Kennel Club Year Book* Part III: Rules and Regulations, at a very modest price direct from the Kennel Club (address on p.76).

4

Heelwork and Sit

The Heelwork and Sit exercises are so closely interrelated that they are best taught simultaneously. Neither should provide any difficulties if you have carried out puppy education in the manner suggested in Chapter 2.

Heelwork is the basic control and disicipline exercise. It has great practical application in that it instils instant obedience, and teaches the dog to walk by your side in a neat and orderly fashion, neither swinging away from you on the one hand nor tripping you up on the other, and then to sit quietly when you stop. If you stop to talk to someone, he is not jumping up or winding his lead round your legs, sniffing around or generally making a nuisance of himself. For competitive work the rules state the dog should be approximately level with, and reasonably close to, the handler's left leg at all times. In reality, to do well even in the Beginners' Class the dog must not only give you his complete attention, but must be seen to do so by carrying his head high and slightly turned round your left leg, looking upwards at you (see pl. 3).

Heelwork begins with the dog sitting close to your left leg. You hold his lead in your right hand with your right elbow bent at 90 degrees. There should be just sufficient slack in the lead to enable it to be taken up and the slip-chain tightened round his neck by the twist of your right wrist. To start the exercise three things happen simultaneously. You say REX . . . HEEL, flick the lead slightly and step off with your left foot. Your dog will have done some puppy-walking on his lead and flat collar, so he will have some idea of what is required of him. If he pulls forward or sideways away from you, correct him by simultaneously saying HEEL in a very firm voice and pulling him in towards you. Immediately he comes in, release the slip-chain and praise him (GOOD BOY, etc.) in a very warm friendly tone. As previously mentioned, you must get into the habit of changing your tone of voice immediately – harsh . . . friendly . . . harsh . . . friendly, and so on. In the long run this is a much more powerful form of control than the lead. Remember only to tweak the slip-chain sufficiently hard to accomplish the required result. You are the Boss but you must be a fair and kindly one. Most dogs, with the exception of the really dominant hard cases, will resent being pulled about too much on the slip-chain and some could be put off obedience-training completely. This is one of the reasons for the 'know your dog' rule; ascertain just how much correction he requires and apply no more than that.

If he has a tendency to lag behind, tugging his lead will probably have an adverse effect. Just give the lead a little flick and pat your left thigh and say HEEL, but this time in an encouraging voice. (Note that the voice is again the main aid.)

If you are unfortunate enough to have a persistent puller, particularly if he is a big, powerful animal, you can reinforce your slip-chain correction by turning sharply right when he is almost at the extent of his lead, and then keeping on walking. Such tactics require more slack in the lead, to which you give a hefty jerk instead of a mere flick of the wrist. You will soon get the idea. We have counselled you not to over-correct the normal, reasonably submissive dog, but a persistent puller must learn the lesson for his own long-term good as well as yours, so don't be afraid to use some power on him. It is a question of being cruel to be kind. A little pain now is far better than a lifetime of pulling and consequently half-choking for ever more.

Once he has got the idea of walking close to you, encourage him to keep in even closer, mainly by using a pleasant tone of voice, alternatively admonishing him reasonably sternly if he tends to move away or loses concentration, and then praising again, until you can walk together with a permanently slack lead. This not only requires good heelwork from your dog, but good footwork from you. In fact some dog-training schools give their human pupils lessons in deportment before they allow them anywhere near their dogs. Walk upright, don't bend over, take reasonably short steps, obviously modifying your stride to the size of your dog. Walk in a lively, natural manner and in a perfectly straight line, and don't waver about. Do not worry about turning corners initially. Go round in an arc and then carry on walking in a straight line. When your dog has grasped the general idea, tighten up your turns gradually until you are going through precisely 90 degrees. Do all right turns at first, progress later to the more difficult left turns, and finally to the right-about and left-about turns, which must be through exactly 180 degrees.

Now you are turning on the spot, wavering to neither right nor left. The dog pivots round you in the right turns and you pivot round him in the left turns. If you walk properly, your dog will soon learn to follow your turns almost as if he is tied to your left leg. He will have the confidence of knowing that you always do precisely the same thing, and that you will not kick him or walk on his feet in the process – nothing is more calculated to make a dog walk wide. In this context it does help if you wear soft shoes for heelwork because then you at least lessen the effect if you do tread on his toes. I have suggested that you hold the lead in your right hand, and in the vast majority of cases this is preferable, but if you find you get better results using your left hand, then do so. However, a good compromise is often to hold the lead in your right hand, thereby allowing you to correct him more easily if he pulls away from you, but at the same time running it loosely through your left hand held low down where the lead joins the slip-chain. This will enable you to correct him if he tends to work too far ahead of you, or to keep him close in left turns.

Another useful training option if your dog continues to work too far ahead of you is to pass the lead behind your back while still holding it in the right hand. This causes an automatic check on him with every step you take.

So far we have talked only about heelwork, but obviously he cannot start from the sitting position unless he learns to Sit. He should know what SIT means from his puppy education, and now he must incorporate it into the heelwork exercise. A dog will normally assume a correct Sit position when your right foot comes up to the left foot. So give the SIT command in a sharp, clear voice as your left foot hits the ground, and halt by closing your right foot to your left foot. He should now be sitting with his front legs in line with your legs, and almost touching them. He must be taught to sit quickly, straight and upright. In other words he must be smartly precise.

The Sit is another exercise in which it is most advantageous for you to practise your footwork without your dog. If you practise in the garden, your neighbours may look a little askance at you, but never mind. You will see what I mean when I describe the actions you take in teaching the Sit. Three things happen simultaneously. As you halt by closing your right foot to your left foot, raise the dog's head by bringing your right hand smartly up to the level of your left shoulder. Most dogs will sit automatically when the head is raised in this fashion. However to make certain, and to ensure a smart Sit in the correct position, push his rump down with your left hand, at the same time pulling him in so that he sits straight and close. Ideally you should not lean over your dog, so if you are agile enough to do the 'knees bend', crouch down in the manner shown in pl. 4 when beginning to teach the Sit. Once the dog is steady in the Sit position, stand up slowly. Praise him quietly, just enough to let him know you are pleased with him, as he may well interpret effusive praise as the signal to get up again. As soon as he learns to Sit promptly and correctly, you may omit the pressure with the left hand on the rump, merely lifting the lead to raise his head. However, you must revert to the use of the left hand again should he become sluggish or sit in a slovenly manner. To maintain your status as the Boss you must insist on perfection at all times.

Although it is necessary to teach the Sit as part of heelwork, use it very sparingly in the early stages of training. If he is commanded to Sit as a routine part of heelwork he will almost certainly begin to anticipate it and this will make him slow and halting.

Once the dog has learned the SIT command he must act upon it under any circumstances, no matter where he is or what he is doing. He may be close to you or far away, he may be in front of you or behind you, but he must obey. For example, you will often require him to Sit at the approach of other animals. A dog feels very disadvantaged if commanded into the Down position in the presence of other animals and consequently resents the command, but this does not apply to the Sit. Thus it is most useful under such circumstances.

When using commands off-lead, hand-signals reinforce vocal commands and also make them more easily learned. Ultimately either the visual or vocal commands may be used alone. The hand-signal for the SIT command is the right hand raised, palm uppermost from waist level to the left shoulder. This is, of course, the same movement you made when you raised his head using the lead, and he will readily recognize this.

When he is quite competent at Heel on Lead, you may start Heel Free. This is identical to Heel on Lead with one most important difference: you no longer have a lead with which to control him. This should present no problem if he has been working well on a slack lead, and Heel Free is not attempted before he is ready for it. Replace his lead immediately, and correct or re-train him if mistakes occur.

Finally, here are two more particularly useful commands which dogs very quickly learn through use. One is CLOSE, which literally means 'Get closer to me'. It is used, for example, if a dog is walking wide during heelwork, particularly on turns, or is too far away in the Sit. The dog must be made to do the work himself. If you always pull him closer to you, he will get used to your moving him, and never make the effort to do it himself. So pat your thigh and command CLOSE, urging him to get himself into the correct position.

The other command is WATCH ME and is used whenever a dog loses his concentration. You will find it particularly useful if he is distracted and looks away from you during heelwork.

Heelwork is the cornerstone of all future training so keep lessons short and have frequent breaks for play. Don't bore him or yourself. Use plenty of praise and encouragement. It is the quality of the heelwork which counts, not the quantity.

5

Down

DOWN is probably the most essential command of all, and is used under many different circumstances. It is the first command the shepherd teaches his dog because of its importance for control. Also it is another way of emphasizing to the dog that you are the Boss. Incidentally, I am going to refer to the dog as 'her' in the next few chapters to break the monotony, and to demonstrate that I am not a male chauvinist, but I shall continue to use the word 'dog' in its generic sense.

The Down is not a difficult exercise to teach, but for a short while it can involve a bit of a wrestling match with a big, reluctant dog. The only requirement is to get her down on her stomach, and make sure she remains there until released.

There are a number of ways of achieving this. Probably the easiest is to start with the dog in the Sit position with you facing her right side. Hook the fingers of your right hand through the slip-chain under her neck, and pull downwards giving the command DOWN in a harsh voice. With a larger dog you can increase the downward pressure by pushing down simultaneously with your left hand on her shoulders (see pl. 5). Hold her down all the time she struggles but when she submits, if only for a few seconds, praise her and release her.

As soon as she looks steady in the Down position, gradually stand up and praise her very quietly and gently, just to let her know you are pleased with her. You are praising her for staying down, so the praise must be given while she is still down. If your praise is effusive and excited, she may well

1 Making up the slip-chain

2 Putting on the slip-chain
   . . . the correct way

3 Heel on lead . . . (Close to left leg; paying full attention; lead
   slightly loose)
   (a) Left view   (b) Right view

4 The Sit . . . (Lead taut above head; left hand pressing down
   and in)
   (a) Rear view   (b) Side view

5 The Down: one method . . . (Pull down with fingers of right
   hand; press down on shoulders with left hand)
   (a) Before   (b) After

6　The Down:
　　alternative method

7　Teaching the Sit . . . Wait

8　The Recall . . . Sit at Present
　　(a) Rear view

(b) Side view

(a)

(b)

(c)

9 The Recall hand-signal . . . (Fast fluid movement; flick hands
   open and back again)

10 The Recall . . . Guiding the dog in for a straight Sit
   (a) Front view   (b) Side view

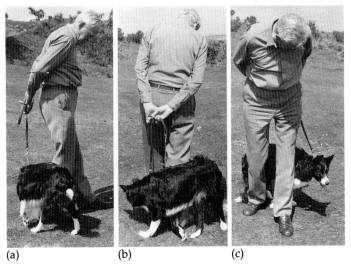

(a)   (b)   (c)

11 Teaching the finish . . . (Dog passing behind handler from Sit
   at Present to Sit at Heel in one smooth movement)

12   The Retrieve . . . forcing the dog to Hold (Gently squeeze
loose skin against teeth and roll dumb-bell in)
(a) Front view   (b) Side view

13   The Retrieve . . . Dog at the Present (A nice straight Sit)
(a) Rear view   (b) Side view

14 The Sendaway . . . Setting him up (Focus his eyes on the
    target area with 'blinkers')
    (a) Side view

(b) Front view

15 The Sendaway . . . a good Down inside the box

16 Distant Control . . . restricting movement

interpret it as a premature release signal. In common with all other exercises, take your time teaching the Down and sound, steady progress will result.

An alternative method, particularly for a larger and more reluctant dog, is to do as I have suggested with the left hand but instead of pulling the slip-chain down with the right hand, pass the lead attached to the chain under the instep of the right foot and pull upwards on the lead (see pl. 6). The dog may be held in the Down position by standing on the lead near the slip-chain. Another slight variation instead of passing the lead under the instep with the foot flat on the ground is to stretch the lead out parallel with the ground and about twelve inches above it, then holding it firmly in the right hand place your foot on the lead, push your foot down to the ground and hold it there.

A further alternative, with the dog still in the Sit position, is to sweep her front legs forward with your right forearm, still pressing down with the left hand on the shoulders.

I have described the Down from the Sit because that is the easiest way to teach it initially. Once she understands the command she must be taught the Down from the Stand.

Immediately you no longer require your hands to force her into compliance you can use them to make the Down hand-signal. This will reinforce the verbal command and considerably assist the response time. The hand-signal must be very emphatic, and is made by sweeping the fully extended right arm from shoulder height to near ground level, with the palm downwards.

The Down exercise must be progressed until she goes down immediately, whether on lead or off, and whether by your side or hundreds of yards away. Even if she is running at full stretch, she must be taught to go down as if her legs had been scythed from under her. She must go down when commanded no matter whether she is moving away from you or towards you. However, practise the Down coming back to you (usually known as the 'Drop on Recall'), only very occasionally, otherwise she will become very sluggish in returning to you as she will be anticipating the Down command.

Many dogs have been saved from death or serious injury in traffic or other hazardous situations by being taught immediate response to the Down command. Many more could have been saved if their owners had only bothered to train them.

Your dog now responds to the SIT and DOWN commands. Next she must be taught to remain in these positions when so instructed.

6

Wait, Novice Recall and Finish

This is very much a 'building block' exercise because it is taught in three separate parts and then put together at a later stage. It is another very practical exercise, because it teaches your dog to Sit and Wait and later Down or Stand and Wait while you move away from her, and then to rejoin you immediately upon command.

WAIT

Many obedience exercises are contradictory, as though we seem determined to confuse the poor dog. We have just taught her to walk close by our side. Now we are going to move off and leave her. She won't be all that keen on the idea at first so be patient with her and proceed very slowly. Start with her in the Sit position on your left. Hold the lead reasonably taut above her head in your left hand with the slip-chain at the back of her neck. Give the command WAIT in a firm but friendly voice, remembering what I have said about just how much you can convey by your tone. Also elongate the vowel, WAAAAAIT. Take a slow pace to the right, pause for a second or two and return to her side. Praise her quietly for staying. If she attempts to move, repeat the command and hold her in position by the lead in your left hand. Repeat this once or twice, gradually taking the tension off the lead. Now progress the exercise by taking one step to the right, and then moving slowly round to the front, and then back again, checking her if necessary with the lead in the left hand and repeating the WAIT command (see pl. 7). Then build the exercise up still further by taking a pace to the right, then walking slowly right round her and resuming your place by her right side.

At the next lesson, if she now remains steady, use a lead extended by a piece of light line and held in the right hand. Give the WAIT command and introduce the associated hand-signal, being the palm of your left hand placed just in front of her face. Move forward slowly, stepping off with the right foot. Move away two or three paces, turn slowly. Pause, return slowly to your dog, stand right in front of her and pause again. Do not let her move. Now walk round her and again finish by standing with her on your left. Practise the exercise gradually moving further and further away from her and paying out the extended lead. Don't forget to step off with the right foot when you don't want the dog to accompany you as opposed to the left foot when you do.

NOVICE RECALL

There are two types of Recall in competitive obedience. However, for the purposes of pet dog-training we need concern ourselves only with the Novice Recall. Details of the other version, called the 'A' Recall, are included in the Advanced section of the book (p.104) for those who wish to progress to the more complex exercises.

Once your dog is steady in the Wait while you move away from her on an extended lead, you can start teaching the Recall. With her sitting in front of you, give the command BESS ... COME in a very pleasant and welcoming voice, and start collecting the lead in as she comes towards you. After her puppy education she will probably come to you most willingly, but if she is a bit slow, encourage her both vocally and with the lead, but don't haul her in. Once she gets the idea of returning from a few paces away, give her the SIT command as she reaches you, so that she is sitting squarely in front of you (see pl. 8). Now practise the Recall and the Sit over a short distance without the aid of the lead, but substituting a hand-signal to augment the voice command. The Recall hand-signal requires the use of both hands which are folded in front of you, palms inwards, with straight arms. They are then flicked open to expose the palms and then flicked back to their original position (see pl. 9). If there are any problems she must be put back on her lead and re-trained. Titbits should not be necessary but may be used temporarily and very sparingly to accelerate a tardy Recall.

Incidentally I suggest the voice-command COME rather than HERE as the latter can easily be confused with HEEL.

Gradually increase the distance over which she must return, and insist on a straight Sit with her looking up at you. You can always give her a second chance by taking a pace back and calling her in again.

The handler can greatly assist his dog into a straight Sit by standing correctly. His feet should be about twelve inches apart and pointing straight forward. He must never move his feet to accommodate the dog. She must learn to position herself correctly. The handler must also stand upright, keeping his body still and not bending over.

The most usual reason for a crooked Sit is the dog's failure to come in straight. This fault can be prevented quite simply by either of two methods. Probably the easiest is to stick your right foot out if she is coming in offset to your right, or the left foot if her return has a bias to the left. This is usually enough to correct her, but it is recommended that you use the command STRAIGHT simultaneously. She will soon learn the meaning of the word as applied to both sitting squarely in front of you or in the Heel position.

The second method of encouraging a straight return and Sit is to guide the dog in with your hands. This method can either be used alone or in conjunction with that described above. As you know, most dogs will follow hands, so guide her in with both hands held flat, palms down and thumbs linked and arms fully extended. The movement is almost as if you are pulling her in on a pair of reins. It is rather difficult to describe but very easy to do. Pl. 10 will assist you. The STRAIGHT command should be given with this method also.

I said earlier that as the dog assumes the Sit position she should look up at you. This is also easy to achieve by keeping her continued attention on your hands. These finish in the same position whether they have been used for the Recall signal or to guide her in. So, as she sits, raise both hands up to waist level and her eyes will follow them (see pl. 8).

I am sure you have got into the habit by now, but don't forget to praise her well for carrying out your command or even for making the attempt.

THE FINISH

The Finish is merely the dog completing an exercise by moving round you from the Sit in front to the Sit at Heel position. There are two methods of achieving this, but for the purposes of pet dog-training I will describe the most common one.

With the dog sitting in front of you, in what is usually called the Present position, hold her lead in your right hand with the slack gathered in, and the slip-chain at the back of her neck. Give the command HEEL and take a step back with your right foot. This should encourage the dog to get up and follow your right leg. Ease her round the back of your legs, transferring the lead to the left behind your back in the process (see pl. 11). Give the SIT command when she is in the correct Heel position by your left leg. Close the right foot back to the left foot. Praise her well. You will appreciate that the movement of the right foot is only for training purposes and should be discontinued once the Finish has been learned. She should move round your legs as rapidly and as close as possible, and the command CLOSE is as applicable here as it is for heelwork. Once again the Sit must be immediate and straight. When she is competent the lead may be removed.

With the lead off, the hand-signal to be used for the Finish, to reinforce the command HEEL, is the open right hand flicked round the right thigh.

You should teach and practise the Wait, Recall, and Finish separately, and ultimately combine them into one exercise, always with the advantage that one element may subsequently be practised or corrected in isolation if necessary. Don't forget that it is essential to revert to re-training on the lead if a fault occurs or an exercise becomes slovenly with the lead off.

7

The Retrieve

Don't play tug-of-war with a puppy if you want her to retrieve properly, but do encourage any natural tendency she may have to carry things about and bring them back to you. Many dogs derive great pleasure from retrieving and in some the instinct is very strong indeed. So much the better, but even so, proper instruction is still necessary to ensure a reliable Retrieve every time. You will readily see, however, that by teaching the Sit, Wait, Recall, Sit at Present and Finish, she already knows much of the Retrieve exercise.

While she is very young and still playing at the exercise, any suitable retrieve object will do, for example, a piece of cloth with a knot tied in the middle. However, I do recommend that you purchase the universal wooden dumb-bell for serious training, as she will need dumb-bell experience for some of the obedience tests should you subsequently decide to compete. Do ensure that the dumb-bell you buy is of a suitable size and weight for your dog and that the square ends are sufficiently large for the dog to be able to pick it up easily without scraping the ground with her lower jaw.

First she must be taught to accept the dumb-bell in her mouth. If, as a puppy, she has been encouraged to carry things around, there will probably not be much problem. Sit her on your left side, with her lead on, half-turn towards her and kneel on her lead. Alternatively, sit on a box or low chair with her in front of you and with your foot on the lead, as you need to keep her very close. Offer her the dumb-bell by holding it close to her nose and give the command BESS . . . HOLD. If she will take it with a little encouragement, all well and good. If not, she must be forced to do so, because you have reached a stage from which there is no turning back. She must take and hold the dumb-bell before this lesson is over. She must *never* be allowed to disobey a command. If she will not accept the dumb-bell willingly, you must open her mouth and gently roll the dumb-bell in, repeating the command BESS . . . HOLD very firmly.

To open her mouth, place your left hand over her muzzle and gently squeeze the loose skin against her teeth (see pl. 12). The usual rule applies, use only the amount of force necessary to achieve the objective. When the dumb-bell is in her mouth, hold her head up by placing your right hand under her jaw to ensure she does not spit it out and stroke the back of her head with the left hand. Praise her and make a great fuss of her while she is holding it. If you praise her after she has either given up the dumb-bell or spat it out, she will naturally assume she has been praised for that rather than for holding it.

I have made all this sound very simple. Sometimes it is and at other times it is a bit of a fight, but it is one you must win. I said at the outset that you must be obeyed – every time. When using force to teach a young dog to hold, be very gentle and very careful both in making her hold and in removing the dumb-bell from her mouth. Some dogs are more easily persuaded to hold the dumb-bell if the centre bar is covered by sewing a cloth or thin pad round it. It is, of course, an added protection against accidentally damaging her mouth, but it should be removed as soon as practicable.

When she has held the dumb-bell more or less willingly for a few seconds, issue the command GIVE, and remove it from her mouth. If it has been a struggle, have a game with her and end the training session on a happy note. If, as sometimes happens, she is reluctant to give the dumb-bell up, you can force her to do so by poking your forefinger into her mouth just behind the dumb-bell. This is quite painless for you both and can be used to make her release anything she is holding. In fact, if it is a small object, with your hand under her jaw you can insert a forefinger in one side of her mouth and your thumb in the other.

Once she will accept the dumb-bell readily and hold it for a while without spitting it out, start holding it further and further away from her, so that she has to stretch for it and subsequently has to get up and move towards it. Give the HOLD or HOLD IT command each time and praise when she takes the dumb-bell. Continue like this until she will pick it up off the ground, either from a stationary position or while she is walking towards it. A dog is often encouraged to hold the dumb-bell if, after she has picked it up, she is then walked round on her lead with it in her mouth, possibly with you providing quiet insistence by placing your hand under her jaw.

Now try a basic sort of Retrieve. Have her standing or sitting on your left and throw the dumb-bell a very short distance. Release her, simultaneously giving her the BESS . . . HOLD command in a very excited voice. Hopefully she will pick it up, so now encourage her to return to you by calling her name in an urgent voice. Do not call before she has picked it up as otherwise she may decide to return without it. If she does not pick it up, revert to lead-training. Alternatively, try running up with her on the lead once you have thrown the dumb-bell and encouraging her to pick it up. Don't pick it up yourself and give it to her – she must do it herself.

Another mistake which often occurs is that a dog picks up the dumb-bell and fails to return. If she has this tendency, start running backwards, calling her name in an excited voice, immediately after she has picked up the dumb-bell and turned towards you. There is always at least one exercise which every dog finds difficult, and for which the usual training methods are not effective. So the handler must analyse the problem and be innovative in devising a solution.

The Retrieve can sometimes be one such exercise for which a little ingenuity is required. This is one of the fascinations of dog-training.

Once she will retrieve the dumb-bell satisfactorily, the complete exercise can be put together. Start with her sitting on your left and tell her to WAIT. She has already learned this command, but she may need restraining initially because of the excitement of retrieving the dumb-bell. So until she gains a little more experience hook a couple of fingers of your left hand in her collar as you throw the dumb-bell. Pause for a few seconds, then give the BESS . . . HOLD command and release her. Encourage her to return fast, if necessary running backwards and slapping your thighs in excitement. Give her the SIT command as she comes in front of you. She has already learned this command so you must ensure that not only does she sit straight in front of you, but also lifts her head to present the dumb-bell to you without mouthing it (see pl. 13).

Remember to use all the aids to ensure a straight return and Sit as I have already described for the Recall. After all this is only a Recall with a dumb-bell in her mouth. However, if her Sit is still crooked, necessitating your taking a step back and calling her in again, remove the dumb-bell before you do so.

Now tell her to GIVE and remove the dumb-bell carefully from her mouth. Complete the exercise with the Finish, as described in the previous chapter.

I referred above to mouthing. This is chewing on the dumb-bell, or indeed any other Retrieve article. It is a bad habit but a very common one and it must be stopped immediately it begins. Many dogs will retrieve some objects perfectly but 'mouth' others. I start to correct the fault by repeating the command HOLD in a stern voice. If this does not have the desired effect, I say NO, pause and then repeat HOLD in an uncompromising tone. At worst I have had to use the reprimand BAD DOG in the most menacing tone I can muster.

If you have ambitions to enter competitive obedience, it will be necessary, at a later stage, to teach your dog to retrieve all manner of objects. The Beginners Class allows a Retrieve with any article provided by the handler and the next two grades specify that a dumb-bell must be used. However, the two highest grades require a dog to retrieve any article supplied by the judge, subject to certain qualifications. Don't start practising with other articles too soon, thereby confusing your dog or spoiling her dumb-bell Retrieve.

It takes some time to perfect the Retrieve but it is a very attractive and polished exercise when properly executed and is excellent for control and discipline. It is also one which most dogs enjoy hugely as well as exercising their minds.

Just one word of warning. Break off all other training when teaching the Retrieve. Teach it as a separate short session. If you do your normal training in the morning, teach the Retrieve in the afternoon.

8

Sit and Down Stays

SIT . . . STAY

The initial training for the Sit . . . Stay is very similar to that
already detailed for the Sit . . . Wait. For that reason you
should have not the slightest problem with it. The essential
difference between the two is that the WAIT command means
'Pause because I am going to give another command or call
you to me', while the Stay command means, 'Stay where you
are and don't move until I come back to you'. Commence
training with the dog sitting on your left with you holding the
lead slightly taut above her head in your left hand. Give the
command SIT . . . STAY (again elongate the vowel STAAAAY), in
a firm but friendly voice. Take a slow pace to your right, and
then back again, checking her with the lead if she attempts to
move. Praise her well for staying. Repeat the exercise, gradually reducing the tension on the lead and increasing the time
and distance you move away. Move to the right and to the
front, then move round her just as you did in the Wait
training. Then repeat the exercise with her lead removed.
Don't forget to step off with the right foot to indicate to her
that she must not follow you.

The object of this exercise is that you can leave her and go
out of her sight and she will remain motionless in the full
confidence that you will return to her, no matter how long
you are away. This does not mean you should leave her
outside shops or in any other dangerous situation without

tethering her. So now the exercise progresses with you leaving her in the Sit position and going just outside the door and then returning again almost immediately, and quietly praising her for staying. Absent yourself for gradually longer periods but keep her under covert observation until you are certain of her reliability. Practise the Sit . . . Stay under all sorts of conditions, both inside and outdoors. For example, when in the park, make her Sit . . . Stay while you hide behind a tree or the groundsman's hut. Keep her under observation, and in the earlier stages of training pop back into view very briefly every so often.

DOWN . . . STAY

This should be simplicity itself. She already knows the commands DOWN and STAY, so train precisely as you did for the Sit . . . Stay, but with her in the Down position. If she does move in any of the Stay exercises while you are out of her sight (but not she out of yours), return to her quickly but quietly and replace her as she was, in the Sit or the Down, and in exactly the same spot. This is most important. She should be reprimanded for moving in a low voice, but one which leaves her in no doubt she has done wrong. In the earlier stages of training a dog will often get up and come to find you. This is natural but must be stopped immediately. The most frequent subsequent fault is that she will change her position, for example, from the Sit to the Down, and this must also be corrected immediately.

When returning to your dog after a Stay, it is advisable to refrain from looking her straight in the eye as this unsettles some dogs, who interpret it as a premature release signal. She should remain absolutely still, with you standing on her right, until you tell her she may move.

For obvious reasons don't teach the Recall and the Stays at the same session. Teach one in the morning and the other in the afternoon or next day. If, when she is much more experienced, you practise them at the same session, do a little heelwork in between to break the dog's train of thought and thereby avoid confusion in her mind.

9

Stand, Stand . . . Stay and Temperament Test

STAND

Most exercises taught in this book have a practical purpose, and the Stand is no exception. There are many occasions when you want her to Stand – to be brushed or towelled down, to be examined, to have her muddy paws dried and so on.

To teach the Stand, commence with the dog in the Sit position with you facing her right side. Hold her lead in your right hand shortened down almost to the slip-chain and with all the slack gathered in. Give the command JILL . . . STAND in a pleasant voice, elongating the vowel, STAAAAND. Simultaneously run your left hand lightly down her left flank and as she stands up, finish with the flat of the hand halfway down her left leg very gently pushing the leg back, thereby locking it against the joint. By holding her in towards you with the same hand you will stop her turning sideways as she stands. If at the same time you hold her head still with the shortened lead, a good Stand should result. Be very gentle and praise her quietly for being a good girl.

There are two methods of teaching the Stand with which I do not agree. The obvious thing is for me not to tell you about them, but I will do so to enable you to be on your guard should someone recommend them to you. One is by putting your foot under the dog's stomach and lifting. For obvious reasons males object to this more than bitches, but either sex can be discouraged for life. The other method is for the handler to pretend to step off with the left foot while the dog is sitting at the Heel position. Yes, the dog will stand all right but will move forward in the process. If you have any ambitions to enter the competitive obedience world, part of one of the tests (called Distant Control) requires the dog to stand from both the Down and Sit positions, without moving forward. Thus it is best to start in the correct way by teaching her to stand by moving her rear feet back rather than her front feet forward. Progress the exercise gradually so that she will stand firstly without the aid of your left hand, then without her lead, and finally with you giving the command from a gradually increasing distance.

STAND . . . STAY

She has already learned the Sit . . . Stay and the Down . . . Stay. Teach and practise the Stand . . . Stay in exactly the same way. Ultimately aim at achieving a two-minute Stand . . . Stay with you in sight, a five-minute Sit . . . Stay and a ten-minute Down . . . Stay, both with you out of sight.

TEMPERAMENT TEST

Frequently people walk up to a strange dog and stroke her, or at least attempt to do so. Or they shoot a hand out to pat her as she passes. In particular, most children are fascinated by dogs and toddle fearlessly up to them. All pet dogs are expected to accept this without resentment. Certainly a dog which exhibits aggression is a liabilty to her owner and a serious potential danger to the public.

It is to be hoped that the dog you have chosen has an impeccable temperament, but whether she has or not, she must be trained meticulously from puppyhood to accept handling. Certainly all dogs are improved by obedience-training and in some cases an indifferent personality can be transformed. To assist the building or consolidation of a good temperament an animal should be treated fairly and with love and consideration from earliest puppyhood. She should permit her food, or bones, or indeed anything to be removed from her without any fuss. She should be socialized with humans and other dogs throughout her life. She should not be teased, particularly by children, or exposed to bullying or frights as a puppy, either by humans or other dogs. She should not be beaten or ill-treated in any way.

There is a formal Temperament Test in the second and third grades of Obedience Classes. In the Novice Class the dog is required to be on her lead with the handler standing by her head. The judge approaches quietly from the front and runs his hand gently down the dog's back. The judge may talk quietly to the dog to reassure her. Not surprisingly, any undue resentment, cringing, growling or snapping is penalized. The test in Class A is basically similar, the major difference being that the dog is off lead. This is a very simple test of a very important matter.

Start formal Temperament Test training with her on her lead in the Stand position. Obviously she must be used to being stroked by her handler before introducing other people, family and friends first and then strangers. The lead can of course be removed at a later stage.

One frequently hears an owner say, 'Oh, she doesn't like children', or, 'Be careful, she hates men'. There is usually a very good reason for such specific dislikes. Maybe she has been teased by children or ill-treated by a man. It may just be that she has been brought up in an exclusively female environment and is nervous of, and therefore mistrusts, men and children. This brings us back to proper puppy education, and temperament training must include handling by men, women and children.

She must be taught to stand still while being stroked, whether on or off lead. Although the official tests specify that the judge shall approach the dog from the front, it is essential that she is taught to expect approaches from any direction. In the real world a child can come up to her from any angle, inside or outside her field of vision.

Unfortunately, no amount of training will make a dog of really bad temperament completely reliable. Do your very best with her, but take no chances whatsoever, particularly with children – don't forget you are legally liable for your dog's every action.

Finally, please don't breed from any dog of unsound temperament, whether the fault is aggression on the one hand or extreme nervousness on the other, no matter how perfect she may be in every other way.

10

What Next?

If your dog is reasonably proficient at all the foregoing exercises and is just as well-behaved and controlled in her daily routine as she is while under training, then you have a good canine citizen and an animal of which to be proud.

All the foregoing exercises have practical applications, and should you now be bitten by the training bug and wish to enter competitive obedience, they also cover all that is necessary for the Kennel Club's Beginners and Novice Classes. These are the first two of the five competitive levels. If you do have such ambitions, I recommend that you not only attend a good training school, but also go to a few shows as a spectator. Much can be learned from books, but training classes are a great additional help at the lower levels and essential for the higher ones. However, remember my earlier advice about not accepting at face value everything instructors tell you. Listen and learn, then make up your own mind on what is right for you and your dog. Remember you know your dog much better than does any instructor, so don't be pressured into doing anything during a lesson that you know is totally wrong for you both. Unfortunately some instructors do use bullying tactics and if you are unlucky enough to meet one like this I suggest you join another club.

It may well be that you wish to advance further with your dog, but do not fancy pure obedience-work, in which case you may consider Agility or Working Trials more appropriate, assuming of course that these are within your dog's capabilities. An Agility course consists of jumps of various kinds, solid and flexible tunnels, the 'A'-frame, the dog-walk, the weaving-poles, the see-saw and so on. It is rather energetic for the handler as well, for although he/she does not have to cope with the obstacles, he/she has to accompany the dog round the course as fast as possible, as scoring is on a faults and time basis, rather like show jumping. I speak with feeling when I say it is pretty hard going for the elderly handler! At the present time not all clubs have Agility sections, but it is a rapidly growing facet of the sport. Some purists denigrate Agility, but it is good fun, good exercise and requires skilful control of the dog. It is very exciting to a dog, and consequently more phlegmatic animals are better suited to it.

One urgent word of warning: never start a dog on any form of jumping training until she is at least a year old. Even then start with very low jumps and build up slowly. Also, never allow a dog to attempt a jump beyond her capability. It is extreme cruelty.

Working Trials are also conducted under Kennel Club Regulations. There are five levels, being Companion Dog (CD) Stake, Utility Dog (UD) Stake, Working Dog (WD) Stake, Tracking Dog (TD) Stake and Police Dog (PD) Stake. The work each competitor is expected to do is divided into different groups, such as Control (Heelwork, Sendaway, Retrieve, etc.), Agility (various types of jumps), Nosework (Searching, Tracking, etc.), and Patrol (for PD Stake only – this is mainly for criminal work).

You can usually obtain the addresses of your local dog-training clubs from such places as the vet's surgery, the pet shop, the police station and the local newspaper. Some clubs are independent, while other are affiliated to the Kennel Club from whom you can obtain not only club addresses but full details of the regulations pertaining to Obedience Classes, Agility and Field Trials. The address is:

The Kennel Club,
1–4 Clarges Street
London W1Y 8AB.

It is necessary for your dog to be registered with the Kennel Club if you intend to participate in Competitive Obedience, Agility or Working Trials. If the animal is already breed-registered you need take no further action, but if not, you should apply for Obedience, Agility or Working Trial registration. For these purposes it does not matter at all if the dog has no pedigree, or indeed if you have no knowledge whatsoever of its breeding or background.

Whatever you decide to do I am sure you and your dog can give each other very much more pleasure than you ever thought possible. It is certainly true that the more you train your dog the closer you become.

11

More Commands, A Few Tips and Some Fun

In this chapter I provide some brief notes to indicate a few more useful commands and the sort of additional exercises and games which you and your dog can enjoy together to your common benefit. I leave it to your imagination to extend these games and to devise new ones. In fact, some of them can be started when your puppy is quite young. You do not have to wait to complete formal training before you begin them.

CURIOSITY

Dogs have a great natural curiosity, and derive immense pleasure from watching the world go by. So let her look out of the patio door or put a special old chair for her under the front room window. Don't shut her away. Indulge this simple and harmless pleasure. A happy and contented dog is the only kind to have.

SPEAK AND STOP SPEAKING

The ideal is to be able to control your dog's barking. This is not difficult, and it is in fact probably easier to teach her to be quiet when told if she will also bark on command. The easiest way to do this is by the natural method I referred to earlier.

When she barks of her own volition, encourage her enthusiastically and excitedly: FLOSS . . . SPEAK, GOOD GIRL, etc. You can create artificially situations in which you know she will normally bark. For example, if she barks when a visitor knocks at the door, then have someone do just that for you when you want to carry out some Speak training. However, be most insistent that she stops immediately you command FLOSS . . . QUIET, in your most authoritative voice. Don't forget the praise. As a last resort in most cases you can stop a dog from barking by simply holding her mouth shut.

STEADY

This is a very useful command which she will learn gradually by usage. She will interpret the calm tone of your voice in which the exhortation is made. It is used under many and varied circumstances, when she is getting over-excited or over-exuberant, or moving too fast and you want to settle or slow her down.

DROP OR DROP IT

Use this or a similar command if, for example, she picks up something undesirable, dangerous or forbidden. Instant obedience is mandatory. She must spit it out as a reflex action. If she looks as if she is about to pick it up again, I use the dual command in a very stern voice, DROP IT . . . LEAVE IT. Unless a dog will give up anything and everything without hesitation you will spend a lifetime pursuing her and trying to separate her from any object she does not wish you to have. This exercise well repays the time spent teaching it.

GUARDING

A vicious or unpredictable dog is an absolute liability. Nevertheless your good-tempered pet dog can give the appearance of a guard-dog, particularly if she is fairly large, when you open your front door to a caller. In any event you do not want her rushing outside barking like a maniac and jumping all over your visitor. If you train her to lie by your feet and remain quite still when you open the door, she will give a passable imitation of a guard-dog, and will certainly make any unwelcome person think twice.

Train her on her lead initially, just as you do with every other exercise. The fact that she has already learned the DOWN and WAIT commands makes this exercise simplicity itself, just another example of your control over your dog.

ROLL OVER

How many times have you seen dog-owners indulge in a contest closely resembling all-in wrestling while trying to turn a dog over to examine or brush her. Most, but not all dogs (very dominant animals hate it) will readily roll over on command once they understand what is required of them. I give mine the command in two parts, DOWN and then ROLL OVER. This is another exercise which starts during puppyhood using the natural method. An alternative with a very dominant dog is to get her to stand still with her forefeet on a box or chair to enable you to reach her underside.

FRONT

Frequently during training you want your dog to move from, say, the Heel position to the Present. So teach her the command FRONT. Bring her in from either side making sure she sits straight in front of you. If necessary, stick out the foot on the side from which she is approaching as you did while teaching the Recall (see p. 59).

BACK

This is another command which adds refinement to your ability to control. It is useful in a number of rather different circumstances. I use it, for example, if my dog is working too far forward during heelwork and I want her to ease back. I also command BACK if she is some distance away from me, either moving or stationary, and I want her to go away from me rather than come towards me.

I also combine it with other commands, such as SCENT . . . BACK, about which more later (see p. 81).

The next three or four suggestions are not strictly exercises but they are instructive as well as enjoyable to most dogs. They indulge the instincts to carry, retrieve and scent; exercising the instincts is always pleasurable to a dog. Furthermore they provide both physical exercise and mental stimulation.

HIDE AND SEEK

Make your walks more exciting. Get someone to hold your dog, or when she is trained, tell her to WAIT. Go and hide and call her to you. This will exercise her ears, eyes and nose, as she will probably use them all to find you. You can make the exercise easy or difficult according to the distance you move away and the extent of your concealment. However, as she becomes more experienced, make sure she has to use her nose much more than the other senses.

Another variation is to hide a ball or her favourite toy, carrying your scent of course, in the garden or in the house and teach her to FIND IT.

Incidentally, she must always be successful in every exercise she undertakes. With Hide and Seek, she must always find you, even if you have to call continuously to guide her to you and then stand in full view. Similarly she must find the ball or whatever you have hidden even if you have to show her where it is.

SCENT . . . BACK

This exercise teaches the dog to follow your scent back over ground you have already covered, to find an article you have dropped. For training I use a variety of objects, starting with something easy like our familiar old friend, the knotted piece of cloth. In reality you may have inadvertently dropped your wallet or your car-keys.

Start by dropping the object just a few yards behind you in full view on the footpath, and send the dog back for it using the SCENT . . . BACK command and pointing backwards. Gradually increase the distance to some hundreds of yards or more, dropping the article in less and less obvious places, thereby forcing her to use her nose. When she is competent at the exercise, introduce other articles for her to find. You must scent all the articles you use by rubbing them in your hands for fifteen seconds or so.

SIMPLE TRACKING

This, another interesting nosework exercise, must be carried out in an area little used by either humans or animals, otherwise your dog will be confused by the multiplicity of their tracks.

In a way, this is the reverse of SCENT . . . BACK, in that, out of sight of your dog, you walk forward to a selected location, hide an object (yes, let's start with the knotted cloth again), return to your starting point and then call your dog up to follow your track, find the object and retrieve it.

Once again you begin by letting the dog see what you are doing. You put her in the Sit or Down ... Stay, walk forward ten or twenty paces, drop the object in full view and return to your dog. Give her the command SEARCH and encourage her to do what virtually amounts to a Retrieve, an exercise with which she should now be thoroughly familiar. Repeat the exercise in this manner, increasing the distance and placing the object in less obvious places, but adjacent to the track, such as in long grass or under a hedge. Don't forget to scent the cloth now that she has to rely on her nose, however minimally. To avoid confusion, always return precisely along the line of your original track.

When she has got the idea, leave her in the car, or some other convenient place well out of sight, and lay a very short track, placing the object in a comparatively easy place for her to find. If you scuff a footmark at the beginning of the track it will encourage her to get her nose down and follow your scent and locate the article. The exercise is progressed by making the tracks longer, with changes of direction and so on. Not all dogs will take to tracking, but it is a strong natural instinct in many breeds, and they will thoroughly enjoy it once they get the idea of what is required of them.

You may be surprised just how good your dog is at tracking, which can be extended into a very exciting exercise by following other people's scents, laid hours before over complicated courses.

CARRYING

Many dogs love to carry things around, so encourage yours to carry a newspaper or some other harmless object. Teach her to take an article to a nominated person in the house or garden with a command like CARRY TO ... GEORGE. As an extension of this exercise try teaching her to fetch your slippers. At the beginning someone will have to be in the bedroom or wherever to give them to her or at least point them out to her, but an intelligent dog soon gets the idea, and will go herself. The more she is made to use her brain the more proficient she will become. Most animals bring one slipper and have to be sent back for the other one, but it is a marvellous moment if, without any prompting from you, she uses her head and suddenly decides to bring you the pair in a single mouthful.

CARE

Books on the care of dogs fill many library shelves, and the subject is not really within the scope of this book, but may I remind you of a few important though rather obvious points.

1 Never leave your dog wet. Particularly, never send her to bed wet. You can save many soaking wet or muddy towels by taking the worst off with an old newspaper, then finish with a rough towel.

2 Daily grooming is essential. Make it an opportunity to use your eyes and your hands to find any lumps, bumps, abrasions, ticks, burrs and so on that need immediate attention. Also check mouth, teeth, paws, pads, and claws.

3 Always have your vet administer the annual booster inoculation against the killer diseases, distemper, parvo virus, virus hepatitis and leptospirosis immediately it is due. Don't delay.

4 Dogs can be affected quite badly by various kinds of stings, but the prompt use of a good antihistamine cream can greatly alleviate the situation. I always keep some handy, both at home and in the car. The incidence of snake-bite in various areas appears to have increased in recent years, and

the immediate use of antihistamine cream together with tablets which your vet can supply, provide effective first aid pending professional attention.

5   Most fit dogs love a game with a ball, but do not use a ball so small she can swallow it. Never use a golf ball, and even a tennis ball is too small for the larger breeds. When in doubt buy a much larger ball. A large, solid, rubber ball is the safest, but even habitually catching one of these loosens a dog's teeth. Perhaps she will accept a rubber ring after all! Personally I always use a stick rather than a ball for water retrieving because the force of the water pushes a ball too far back into the throat and even holding it causes her to open her mouth excessively wide, thereby swallowing a large quantity of water. Conversely, I never use a stick for dry land retrieving or allow my dogs to play with one, because they are highly dangerous. They chew them and swallow small pieces, or get them jammed across the roof of the mouth or between the teeth. Most dangerous of all is the habit all dogs have of occasionally running with a stick held endways on. They can be rushing along and suddenly stub the end of the stick into the ground or some other obstruction thereby pushing it deep down the throat with great force. Invariably the stick breaks leaving a small piece embedded in the throat. I have known some horrific injuries of this kind which, if not fatal, have at best necessitated extensive surgery.

6   Your bathroom scales, your hands and your eyes should all be used to check you are giving her the correct quantity of food for her breed, age, life-style and state of health. A very little adjustment, up or down, can keep her just right.

Regular and sufficient exercise is also essential. Exercise for normal, healthy adult dogs of most breeds should be varied to include normal walking and running, also hard road walking on lead at least twice a week to condition feet, pads and nails and to build muscle. Dogs should be taken to many different places and also encouraged to swim if that is what they enjoy, but not thrown in or otherwise forced if it is against their nature. My own dogs also love to jump on command over such obstacles as park benches. I have already mentioned ball and other games which make exercise much more rewarding and interesting than just going out, and in addition, have decidedly educational value.

7   All dogs need to be well-exercised, well-fed, well-housed, well-groomed, well-trained and well-loved.

With the exception of the most important chapter about 'The Avoidance of Problem Behaviour' at the end of Part I, this is possibly as far as you wish to go, but in the interest of completeness I have concluded this book with a separate section detailing the five advanced tests which must be mastered should you decide to enter competitive obedience beyond the two basic levels. Alternatively, you may wish to teach them to your dog for no other reason than your personal satisfaction. And why not? – I thoroughly recommend that you do.

If you are stopping here, then may I express the sincere hope that my book has helped you achieve a good canine citizen. Have loads of fun with your dog.

12

The Avoidance of Problem Behaviour

In this chapter I am repeating some of the material which was included earlier in the book, but I believe the subject to be so crucial that it must all be assembled under a single heading. Although I am able only to scratch the surface of this vast subject, here are the salient points.

The two factors which dictate all behaviour are heredity (instinct) and environment. Hereditary behaviour occurs either accidentally or as a result of selective breeding. Similarly, environmental conduct is either learned by accident or specifically taught. Thus if you have selected your puppy wisely and trained it properly, then, at least in theory, you should have an impeccably behaved animal. Further, as it is reliably estimated that 70 per cent of behaviour is attributable to environment and only 30 per cent to heredity, the odds are very much in our favour, even if some deficiencies in temperament, which were not immediately apparent, appear later in life.

While many faults or potential character flaws are attributable solely or mainly to either heredity or environment, some are a combination of both. If, in addition, we consider that some hereditary flaws are physical or hormonal in origin, you will readily see that preventive or remedial training may not provide the whole answer. In many cases it does and in practically every other instance it has an essential contributory part to play, but other treatments which only your veterinary surgeon can provide may be necessary to effect a cure. It may be necessary for him to administer drugs (for hormonal imbalance, for example) or surgery (for example castration) may be advisable.

Now let us examine some potential problems and what we can do to prevent them. I have categorized them under just two main headings, for the sake of brevity. They are dominance and fear.

DOMINANCE

The majority of the flaws in temperament are included in this category and most are covered by the term dominance aggression, but the words dominance and aggression are not synonymous. Aggression occurs when dominance is allowed to take over. Dominance is primarily an hereditary factor and as we have already seen, the most dominant dog in the litter is unlikely to make the most suitable family pet. Furthermore, if a dog is allowed to develop his dominant tendencies this begins to involve environmental factors which increase the potential for major problems.

I must digress here for a moment to make a few essential points. First, instinctive behaviour can be eliminated or diminished only by many generations of selective breeding. It can only be suppressed in animals already possessing such instincts.

Second, while dogs are usually more likely to exhibit dominant and consequently aggressive tendencies than bitches, the latter are not immune from this fault. This is because dogs and bitches each have their own pecking order, known to the veterinary profession as dominance hierarchy, and do not share the same social scale.

My third observation is that while it is not surprising that dominance and aggression are more likely to occur in dogs bred for guarding (such as German shepherds, rottweilers, etc.) or fighting (for example Staffordshire bull terriers), size is not the criterion, as many small and toy breeds can exhibit some really nasty behaviour. In these cases it is probably environmental as much as instinctive considerations which are responsible. They are so small and pretty and cuddly that many are subjected to excessive pampering.

Dominance aggression can be directed against both humans and other dogs, anyone or anything not accepting the dominance of the animal concerned. It manifests itself in many ways, such as growling, snarling or biting. The dog will almost certainly resist fiercely any attempt to remove his bone or his dinner or indeed anything from him. Another typical reaction is his aggressive refusal to leave or be removed from his bed (or yours), the settee, armchair, back of the car or anywhere else he views as his territory. Such dogs tend to be loners and want to dictate the sequence of events and the pattern of life. They will not submit to being groomed or examined. They will not permit themselves to be stroked or patted unless they have instigated it. They will indicate to their owner just when they think they ought to be fed or to go out.

Outright aggression apart, they may begin to indulge in what is known in the Services as dumb insolence, and I can think of no better description. The dog will stare you defiantly in the eye. He will either ignore a command, pretending he has not heard it, or react with maddening slowness. Generally he will make it known to his owner that he just does not accept him as the Boss, the pack leader.

I have already counselled you to be ever-vigilant for the first signs of trouble, and problems in this category are most likely to surface just when the dog is beginning to feel his feet, at puberty and at the threshold of adulthood. So what do we do to head off this type of problem if it manifests itself? I have already said that I do not recommend trying to beat the dog into submission, irrespective of his size. If he is a large and very aggressive animal you may well carry a lot of scars for a long time as a result of a confrontation which has got you absolutely nowhere. You still wish to retain his confidence, respect and love, which is the only way for the human–canine relationship to work, but you must strengthen or regain your position as the Boss, so rather more subtlety is needed. You must take steps to reduce the animal's dominance so that you are in full control at all times. The routine is not in the slightest way cruel and should be applied with the correct amount of firmness according to whether he is reasonably submissive on the one hand or a very hard case at the other end of the scale. The whole idea is to cut him down to size and maintain or re-establish strict and willing discipline.

1   Obedience-train him every day, particularly the disciplinary exercises such as heelwork, the Downs and the Stays. Make absolutely sure he obeys instantly every time.

2   If he commences bad habits like worrying for food at table, do not feed him, and do not let any other member of the family feed him. Shut him away from temptation and allow him back into the room only when he will sit quietly in the corner. Reward him only for compliance, but not at the table!

3   If he worries for attention, ignore him. Make a fuss of him only when you wish to do so. Generally never let him initiate any act such as feeding or going out. You must dictate at all times. Don't let anyone else spoil him either.

4   Make him sit and wait when you put his meal down until you tell him he can have it. Don't tease him with a long wait but make him understand he cannot have it until you tell him so.

5   If the problem is one of resistance to removal from beds, settees or armchairs, deny him access to rooms housing these objects until control of the animal is re-established and he will remain on the floor. Initially he must be removed from the furniture but do so by tipping him off or pulling him off with the bed-cover. Do not let it develop into a fight between you.

6   Never let him precede you through a door or gate. Either allow him to follow you at heel or make him sit and wait until you have gone through and then call him. Make him sit again while you shut the door or gate. Similarly insist that he only gets in or out of the car on your command.

7   Never avert your gaze from the stare of a dominant dog – stare him out instead.

8   Never let an animal exhibiting any signs of dominance get up on your lap, or your bed. It seems that the higher he gets from the ground relative to you the more his sense of superiority increases.

9   Never play any 'fighting' games with your puppy and never permit him to play such games with another dog.

10   Pay attention to him only as a result of a submissive act. Totally ignoring an act or an advance made by a dominant dog is much more effective than reprimanding him. He will interpret a reprimand as an acknowledgement, so his aim has been at least partially achieved.

11   Socialize him with people (men, women and children) and other dogs. Insist that he remains steady when being groomed, patted or stroked and when approached by friends and strangers alike. This may well be a very gradual conditioning process with a particularly dominant animal and impossible until you have re-established complete control over him.

12   Be as strict as necessary in your training, but be fair, just and consistent.

There is one other quite common form of aggression which I must include before I leave the subject, and that is chasing. Not surprisingly, this behaviour is strongest in animals selectively bred as predators, such as greyhounds, whippets, lurchers and some terriers, but most breeds have the instinct somewhere in the background and can soon revive it given the opportunity. In an earlier chapter I stressed that all puppies should be trained to ignore all moving objects, human, animal or inanimate. Running children, joggers, cats and bicycles are all very tempting but he must not be permitted to chase anything. There is no short cut. Training must be persevered with, on lead until the animal is quite reliable with anything that moves, no matter how close the dog is to the temptation. Don't forget instincts cannot be eradicated, only suppressed.

Sheep-chasing is a very powerful instinct and an all too common problem. If a dog has developed this habit beyond the scope of normal remedial training there is no alternative but to keep him away from sheep or on a lead in their presence.

I understand that a remotely controlled device which emits a high frequency sound, designed to distract a dog in the act of chasing, is currently being developed by an eminent canine psychologist. It will probably be available by the time this book is published.

Finally, do not hesitate to consult your vet immediately if your dog is not responding to your special training as well as he should or if you have the slightest suspicion that medical or surgical treatment may be required.

FEAR

Instinctive fear certainly exists, but I believe the most common type of fear results when an animal of basically nervous disposition is subjected to traumatic experiences. Thus we can do much to minimize potential damage to a puppy by correct handling and training. Also, as this type of problem behaviour was learned originally, if it is already established in an adult, there is a good chance that it can be reversed.

Fear can be of almost anything – loud noises, traffic, people (men, women or children), insects, other animals and so on.

In Chapter 2 I advocated gradual exposure of the puppy to all the experiences of hectic modern life and I believe this is the best preventive training you can provide. Proceed very slowly, keep a sharp look-out for any indication that a specific fear may be emerging and slant your training accordingly.

We all know that neurotic people create neurotic dogs, so do everything in your power to provide yours with a quiet and peaceful home life. Children rushing about the house and husband and wife constantly bickering do not provide the ideal atmosphere for a nervous dog. Also please remember three of the rules we have already introduced:

1 Never tease a puppy and do not let anyone else do so.

2 Never permit him to be frightened by anyone or anything, and protect him against intimidation by humans or other dogs.

3 Socialize him thoroughly with other animals and men, women and children.

If you have a dog which suffers the anguish of fear you must first isolate him from whatever triggers that fear. When he has recovered his composure, training can commence. He can be exposed gradually and progressively to the mechanism creating the fear. He should be as composed as possible before exposure by soothing, stroking and talking to him in a quiet and relaxed manner. He may be given his favourite titbit during exposure, but do not attempt to comfort him, either verbally or physically, at this critical time as it will only increase his awareness of the triggering factor. It is far better to assume an apparently unconcerned attitude. Of necessity, the process must be very gradual to stand any chance of success. I suppose you can liken it to a man with a fear of heights schooling himself to climb a ladder. He must feel secure on each rung before he attempts the next one and if he tries to proceed too fast he sometimes has to descend a rung to consolidate his confidence.

As before, do not hesitate to involve your vet if necessary as he may consider the temporary use of a mild tranquillizer may help, but don't forget to tell him precisely what you are doing by way of special training.

It is my understanding that British canine psychologists do not subscribe to the 'total immersion' technique as a cure for fear-based behavioural problems as do some human psychologists. This basically involves exposing the patient frequently and suddenly to large doses of whatever triggers the fear sensation. Presumably the rationale is that ultimately the patient will realize that there really is nothing to worry about after all. Personally I cannot see that this technique is much help to man or beast. I cannot conceive taking a gun-shy dog to a bonfire night firework party and expecting a cure. So I do entreat you not to attempt treatment of that kind, no matter who suggests it.

There is one aspect of fear which differs somewhat from the type I have been considering, although the general method of prevention or treatment is very similar to that already described. This is agitation or anxiety which can be triggered by many things such as strange people or places, or separation from the owner. The dog may become restless or excited, he may bark or whine. The problem behaviour frequently extends to his defecating or urinating by day in his owner's absence or when he is shut away alone at night. Alternatively he may be destructive under these same circumstances.

If you are unfortunate enough to see these problems begin to emerge it is vital that you do not lose your temper and punish the poor animal. He has troubles enough and punishment will only exacerbate them. The fact that he urinates on the floor or tears something up is not his way of getting back at you for leaving him alone or shutting him up. The canine mind is not that spiteful.

It is essential that you establish the cause of the behaviour and separate the dog from it initially. For example, if he is destructive when you are out of the house, try taking him with you for a while or leave him with someone. Then start leaving him alone again, but initially for very short periods, and gradually increase them. If he urinates at night when left alone, try permitting him to sleep in his basket in your bedroom for a time and then gradually re-introduce him to the kitchen or wherever he normally should sleep. I know this is completely contrary to the advice I gave earlier about not allowing your puppy to sleep in your room, but this is a special and completely different circumstance. This is presuming that there is no physical reason for such behaviour and that the dog is generally considered to be house-trained in every other respect. In other words, there is a definite and specific reason for his behaviour.

If, for example, it is your absence which appears to trigger it off, one experiment which is well worth trying is to have much less to do with the dog for a while. Have another member of the family feed, groom, exercise and care for him, thereby transferring his reliance and attention to someone else, at least temporarily. Then gradually return to the old relationship.

I am well aware that there are other possible causes for the behavioural problems discussed here, and other problems I have not mentioned at all. The good news is that if you are vigilant, if you know what warning signs to look for and what action to take if problems do occur, then you are in a position to head off potential trouble before it becomes serious. Further, established problems can be improved on, if not entirely eliminated.

Do keep your dog active, mentally and physically. Do not confine him more than you must. Do not leave him alone frequently or for long periods. Keep him interested in the world around him. Quite a simple formula, really!

Part II

Advanced Training

13

Scent Discrimination

The Scent Test is one of the group of exercises known as nosework and is included in its simplest form in the Kennel Club's Classes A, B and C.

In the Class A test, the dog is required to locate and retrieve one cloth supplied by the judge, but carrying the handler's scent, from a group of six cloths, the remaining five being unscented. All cloths used for the Scent Test should measure about six inches by six inches but not more than ten inches by ten inches. The Class B test differs in that a total of ten cloths are used, with the handler's scent on one and a decoy scent on one other.

The Class C test also uses a total of ten cloths, but the cloth to be discriminated carries the judge's scent, not the handler's, and one or more decoy cloths may be used. As the judge does not personally give his scent to the dog by hand, he scents two cloths, one to be placed in the ring, the other being used by the handler to convey the scent to the dog.

All this sounds very complicated, but fortunately nosework is instinctive to most dogs, who greatly enjoy it for just that reason. The trick is to convey to them just what is expected of them, so proceed very slowly. Although recent rule changes now limit the tests to the use of cloths only, I believe the ideal way of teaching scent is to encourage the dog to discriminate an article of any kind, plastic, leather, rubber, metal, paper, wood etc. (but not glass or food), provided it is both easily portable and safe from other miscellaneous articles. The conversion to cloths can be effected once the dog has learned exactly what scent discrimination is all about.

Thus start by using an article which the dog likes which is soft and easy to pick up. For example what my own dogs enjoy is an old piece of soft leather cloth rolled into a cylinder about eight inches long and tied with a leather thong.

Commence with the dog in the Sit . . . Wait position on your left. Toss the article, which you have scented by rubbing it between your hands for about fifteen seconds, among a few objects which the dog is unable to pick up due to their size or weight. I use such objects as bricks, flower-pots, rocks, large pieces of metal or wood, etc. Give him the SEEK command and let him do what is in effect a Retrieve but using the different command. The Scent Discrimination test, like the Retrieve, requires the dog to return with the article and assume the Present position in front of the handler and then complete with the Finish. However, do not worry about this until later. For the moment, just take the article from the dog and praise him well.

When he is confident, progress the exercise. Cover the dog's eyes with your hands and have an assistant place the article among the other objects, using a pair of tongs or similar, so that only your scent is on it. The article should still be in full view of the dog when you remove your hands. Again give him the command to SEEK. Repeat this exercise until you are sure he understands it.

Thus far he has made more use of his eyes than his nose. So now conceal the article behind one of the large objects to encourage him to use his nose to locate it. By this time he knows what he is looking for, and he is quite familiar with your scent anyway. So now is the time to teach him to take scent from your hand. Do this by holding your hand about an inch from his nose with your fingers slightly spread so the air passes between them.

Scent Discrimination is one of the most delicate exercises, so do not clamp your hand over his nose or otherwise give him the impression you are trying to suffocate him. He will resent it. In fact, when he is more experienced he will probably move his head away slightly when he has taken sufficient scent. Approximately ten seconds is enough so do not over-scent him.

Now repeat the exercise, this time giving him the hand-scent before the SEEK command.

The next step is to replace the heavy articles with all manner of smaller ones which he is quite able to retrieve, items such as the cardboard centres of toilet rolls, cigarette packets, cotton reels, pieces of firewood, small plastic containers, metal and plastic lids from jam-jars and so on. (You will find that you now collect and treasure a load of what you previously considered rubbish!) Most of these items are to be used as 'blanks', so they must not carry any scent whatsoever. Thus all plastic, metal, wooden or cloth items must be washed. Use just plain water with no detergents, and wear rubber gloves while you are handling them. Washed items should be put out to dry, and any which are not suitable for washing should be thoroughly aired by being placed either outside, or on a window sill, preferably in the sun, for some days. For the want of a better word, these items are now 'sterile' and should remain so by being kept in plastic bags and handled only with tongs. Should they be mouthed by the dog during training, they must be removed, re-washed and re-aired before further use.

Now back to training. With the dog's eyes covered, have someone place the article carrying your scent down with just one sterile item. Offer him scent from your hand and then give him the SEEK command. Repeat the exercise many times, gradually adding to the number of sterile items, up to nine.

The next progression is to replace the original article with a quite different object bearing your scent, again starting with only one sterile object. Gradually build the exercise up by using more sterile objects and different scented objects until he does not know just what he is being asked to find next. Now he is relying totally on his nose.

This is an exercise in which there is little you can do to help once you have sent him out to SEEK. It is important that you remain calm and quiet and above all never chastise him or get annoyed if he picks up the wrong article. This is one time you do not try to prevent him from making a mistake. Do not shout NO if he is about to pick up the wrong article, or even YES to encourage him if he is hesitant about picking up the correct one. He must do it on his own. If he does select the wrong article, let him bring it back, take it from him quietly, but do not praise him. Just say nothing and send him out again.

As with all the other exercises, if he fails a number of times, you must assume that he has not understood what he is to do. So go back to square one and start training from the beginning again.

When your dog begins to get reasonably proficient start including the Present on return and the Finish to round off the exercise.

The next step is to introduce, one by one, sterile objects which are identical to the scented article, until they are all similar. The final Class B stage is to have someone from outside the family introduce a decoy object amongst the sterile ones. Use cloths as a part of the training for the exercise because they are used exclusively in the Class C test and this will aid you in bridging the gap between the two tests.

The next step is to introduce a cloth as the scent article to be discriminated from the selection of sterile objects. Then replace these miscellaneous items with sterile cloths, one by one, until finally the dog is selecting one scented cloth from a total six cloths of which five are sterile. He is now performing the complete Class A scent test.

To progress to the requirements of the Class B test, it is firstly necessary to increase the number of sterile cloths to eight and finally have someone from outside the family introduce one decoy cloth, so that the dog is discriminating from a total of ten cloths, one handler scented, one decoy scented and eight sterile.

It is easy for a handler to confuse his dog without realizing it while teaching Scent Discrimination. If your dog is making good progress and then suddenly goes to pieces it is an almost certain indication that you have done something to confuse him. So be very careful and if he does become confused, try to ascertain the reason and avoid its repetition. Always keep sterile objects uncontaminated and don't hesitate to change them if there is the slightest doubt. Sometimes very competent dogs seem to lose confidence, and having selected the correct article drop it and go and check on the next one, just to be sure. Sometimes they mouth them. In fact they are checking the nose-scent with the mouth-scent. If they start to develop a loss of confidence you can sometimes help by calling their name, with just a hint of urgency, when they have picked up the correct object and before they have a chance to drop it again. Just call the dog's name, nothing more. If this is not effective then it is back to the beginning again to rebuild confidence.

I recently experienced an enormous deterioration of confidence in one of my dogs who was formerly quite superb at scent. This mystified me to start with but I later concluded that I had totally confused her by teaching her the Search required for Working Trials, whereby a dog must work a relatively large square of ground for a number of quite small scented items and retrieve them all. On returning to normal Obedience Scent Discrimination she just could not understand why only one item was scented and was trying to bring all the articles back, one at a time. So it was back to the drawing board with her and I had learned another lesson as well. It was my fault – not hers.

I mention this to illustrate just how easy it is to confuse a dog, not only in this particular exercise, but in any or all of them. It underlines how careful we must be and also the need for constant analysis and appraisal of just what we are doing and particularly why mistakes or imperfections are occurring.

To return to the requirements of C scent, if you have progressed your training as I have suggested, your dog is now capable of finding one scented cloth from a total of ten identical cloths, of which one carries a decoy scent, the others being sterile. He must now learn to work with more than one decoy and also to take someone else's scent, but from a cloth and not direct from a hand. When offering the scent to the dog, the handler must be careful not to confuse him by giving him his own scent together with that on the cloth. Consequently stand a little away, do not bend over him, and present the cloth to the dog by holding the top corners very delicately between the thumbs and forefingers. The cloth may be held just in front of the dog's nose, or draped over it so that he can breathe through it if he does not object to this. Some handlers not only fold the cloth over the dog's nose, but also tuck the lower part of it into his mouth. Presumably this is to enable him to take a mouth-scent as well as a nose-scent. My own opinion is that this practice can easily lead to the mouthing fault I referred to earlier.

Start this final phase of training with just one or two sterile cloths and no decoys, and as he gains confidence gradually increase the number to a total of ten cloths of which at least two are decoys. He has now moved away completely from taking your scent and discriminating your scented object.

Before leaving Scent Discrimination, I must say something about how the articles are arranged for any of the above tests. For Class A they must be in a straight line but for B and C they can be displayed in any pattern the judge fancies, with the proviso that they must always be between two and four feet apart so that the scent from one does not pervade those either side of it. In any event, if an article is heavily scented and there is a slight disturbance of air caused by wind or draught or just by someone moving about, the scent can easily affect articles some distance away. This is yet another potential cause of confusion to the animal.

For tests B and C the articles can be laid in a straight line horizontally, vertically or slantwise. They can be in the form of a cross or a V, T or an L and so on. The most tricky one is a circle.

Most dogs will happily search round the perimeter of a circle, but few will approach the centre, and that is precisely where the scented cloth is usually placed. Thus dogs must be taught to search systematically all manner of patterns, with the scented articles and the decoys being placed in every conceivable position and even the material of the cloths used must be as varied as possible.

You will remember that when you started training your dog in the Scent Discrimination test you used virtually immovable objects to make it impossible for him to retrieve the wrong article. The same principle applies to all the training for this exercise, so that error is eliminated as far as possible. For example, if he has a tendency to retrieve the wrong article when cloths are being used, you should drive pegs into the ground to which all your sterile cloths and decoys should be firmly attached. Alternatively they may be tied to a line stretched across the floor and fastened at each end.

14

'A' Recall

The Recall for the Class A test is very different from the Novice Recall described in a previous chapter, mainly because it occurs while the handler is walking away from the dog, and continues to do so with the dog walking Heel Free until told to halt by the judge.

The exercise starts with the dog either sitting or in the Down at Heel position, at the handler's choice. The dog is told to WAIT and the handler moves off (with the right foot) when commanded by the judge, who then directs the handler in his movements, left turn, right turn, etc. and then to call his dog. The object is that the dog shall re-join the handler, walking at Heel as smartly and precisely as possible, no matter in which direction the handler is walking when the RECALL command is given.

When you begin teaching this exercise, step off smartly, move just a couple of paces and call the dog in with the REX . . . COME command in an excited voice and slapping your left thigh. The aim is to get immediate response from your dog and also to ensure he understands he must assume the Heel position immediately he reaches you. Walk a few more paces smartly and abort the exercise. Do not introduce the Sit at this stage, otherwise you will delay the dog's return to your side. If he tends to be slow in joining you, perform your initial training using a lead. This means you must call him in as soon as you reach the extent of the lead, so it is only a practical aid for the very first stage. Don't forget the praise for the smart execution of the command.

Develop the exercise by moving further away from your dog before calling him. Next, take a left turn just as he is about to join you. When he has accepted this variation, try turning right as he comes up to you. You are teaching him to expect the unexpected. Frequently the judge issues the HALT command just as you are approaching a blank wall or door, a row of chairs or some other similar obstruction. None the less, the dog has to sit just as close and straight as he does for a normal Sit. This may involve considerable practice because most dogs, and particularly the intelligent ones, tend to turn towards you as they sit. This is because they are anticipating a right turn at just the moment you give the SIT command. When I was describing the SIT as part of heelwork earlier in this book, I suggested you teach yourself to halt by bringing your right foot up to the left. If you do this when halting in front of an obstruction, you will reduce greatly this tendency to a crooked Sit.

15

Sendaway, Drop and Recall

This test is part of both Class B and Class C. It requires the dog to leave the handler and to proceed in any direction indicated by the judge and to be dropped by the handler's command at any spot designated by the judge. At the judge's further command, the handler will then call the dog to Heel while walking in any direction indicated by the judge.

This exercise is not nearly as complicated as it sounds. Indeed, most sheepdogs and gundogs in whom the sendaway instinct remains strong, take to it quickly once they understand what they are required to do.

Let us break the whole exercise down into its four component parts. The handler starts with his dog in the Sit and Wait at Heel position. No problem, he already knows this bit. He is then sent away with the command JIM . . . AWAY (or GO if you prefer). I will come back to this part of the exercise in a moment, but at least he is already quite used to going away to retrieve or to bring back a scent object, so it is not entirely new to him. Next he is told to DOWN, and there is nothing new about this either if he has been properly taught to go down immediately he is so commanded, irrespective of the direction in which he is moving. (Incidentally, there is no point in going ahead with the Sendaway if he is not excellent at the Down.) Lastly, he has to perform what is virtually the A Recall as described in the preceding chapter. So the only really new aspect is sending him away without any apparent reason, as there is nothing to retrieve and no articles to be scented.

Let us digress for a moment to consider the spot to which he is to be sent and upon which he is to be dropped. Normally this is marked is some way, the most usual being a box about one and a half yards square demarcated by four posts or cones or something similar. They can in fact be anything and indeed the box can be a triangle and not a square at all. Alternatively it can be an area chalk-marked on the floor, or just a white painted spot. To carry things to the extreme, there need be no visible mark at all. So for competition purposes the dog should be taught to go to any spot to which he is directed by the handler and he should be trained to expect every possible type of demarcation, although the square box is the most common (see pl. 15). I also practise my dogs with such things as a cut-down carpet square and even a yard of rope laid out at right angles to his line of approach, with the object of dropping him immediately behind it. Use anything and everything you can think of. It is also essential that you practise dropping him on a totally imaginary mark.

So much for the target area. Now let us return to teaching your dog to get there. The old-fashioned method, which I still think is the most effective and therefore consider should be tried first, is to start with him on his lead, either sitting or standing on your left, just two or three yards from the box. Give the command ROY . . . AWAY and run up to the box with him. Give him the DOWN command in an urgent voice once he has entered the target area. At this stage it should not be necessary to have to push him into the Down position, but do so if he appears hesitant at first, because he must drop exactly where you direct and that means he must go down immediately. Repeat this routine a number of times, gradually increasing the distance, until he appears to understand exactly what you require of him. Then take his lead off and repeat the sequence, exactly as before, starting off two or three yards away and gradually moving further away.

Now comes the time to send him on his own. Help him to run straight by ensuring that he sits with both his head and body facing precisely towards the box. The other essential is that you cause him to focus his eyes directly forward to the target area by placing your hands either side of his head to form a sort of blinker as sometimes used on horses (see pl. 14). You must, however, remove your hands and stand up straight before sending him away. Again starting near the box, give him the AWAY command and pray! If he does not respond, it is virtually certain that he still does not understand. Do not scold him, but it is back to the drawing-board, so start again with lead attached. This is one of those exercises where the handler must use all of his or her ingenuity to devise ways of helping the dog. For example, it may assist if you train him in a corridor where he has little option but to go straight. Alternatively, use the angle of two walls, one to act as the end wall and the other to form one side of an alleyway, using chairs laid on their sides to close in the other side.

Another method of getting your dog to understand the Away is to teach the exercise as a variation of the Novice Recall. Sit him a couple of yards from the box and tell him to to STAY. Walk through the box, turn at the far end, kneel down and with your hands mark a spot on the floor towards the back of the box, to indicate to him where he is to go down. Give him the COME command and then the DOWN command when he reaches you. Don't forget the praise when he obeys you.

Another method, which you can start at a very early age in preparation for the Sendaway, is to encourage him to go down on to something soft, such as a small square of towelling or the carpet square referred to earlier. At the appropriate time you can start Sendaway training just as described above, but placing the object down as a target area rather than a box. Later, actually place the object inside the box and send him away to drop on to it. Immediately he gets the idea, remove it and send him away to the bare box. However, continue to practise dropping him on his square without a box occasionally so that he does not forget it, because it could well be used in a competition at some future date.

There are other ways of teaching the Sendaway, such as placing food in the box, but I personally do not like this method for a variety of reasons and I am sure you will find one of the three methods I have suggested most effective.

Practise the Sendaway in as many different places as possible, both outside and indoors, using all manner of target areas. Also vary the distance from which you send your dog, otherwise he will get used to moving a fixed distance and will pull up short or hesitate and generally demonstrate loss of confidence.

I referred earlier to the amount of time to be devoted to daily training. However, now you have reached this stage, I anticipate that frequently you are so engrossed that an hour or more can pass almost unnoticed while both you and your dog enjoy polishing and perfecting certain parts of your exercises. You work on the straight Sit, the clean pick-up, the perfect Present, the tight Finish and so on and almost certainly you are still improving your heelwork. You can now understand just what I meant at the very beginning, when I spoke of the fascination of dog-training. You have to experience it to appreciate it.

You begin to appreciate just how close a bond there can be between human and dog, and how a dog's personality can be improved and, in the case of an indifferent personality, completely transformed, by obedience-training. You can also understand how a hill shepherd and his dog, spending so much of their time together in their isolated world, can communicate almost without words.

16

Distant Control

This test features only in Class C, and requires the dog to Sit, Stand and Down at a marked place not less than ten paces from the handler, in any order, on command from the judge to the handler. Six instructions are given, in the same order for each dog. Excessive movement (i.e. more than the dog's length) in any direction by the dog, having regard to its size, is penalized.

The dog starts the exercise with his front feet behind a designated point. No penalty for excessive movement in a forward direction is imposed until the dog's back legs pass the designated point.

The designated point can be a chalk line on the floor, the joint between the floorboards or paving stones, or virtually anything. The six commands are the following, but in any order as directed by the judge:

1	STAND to SIT	4	SIT to STAND
2	SIT to DOWN	5	STAND to DOWN
3	DOWN to SIT	6	DOWN to STAND

The Sit, Down and Stand positions were all taught early in the training schedule and without doubt the dog will be very well versed in them by now through everyday use. The new element is putting them all together in a variable sequence without his moving more than his own body length. Let us introduce a few do's and don'ts.

1 Don't confuse the dog by practising this exercise in the same sessions as the Stays.

2 Do teach and practise elements in pairs and perfect each pair before you put the whole exercise together.

The ideal would be to teach and practise each element separately, but this is impracticable because you must restore the dog to his original position each time to be able to repeat the exercise. So teach the elements in related pairs, for example:

SIT to DOWN – DOWN to SIT

SIT to STAND – STAND to SIT

DOWN to STAND – STAND to DOWN.

3 Do commence all training on a lead. Progress to working off lead but still standing by his side and only move away gradually as he becomes more confident.

4 Do keep each Distant Control training session very short.

5 Do start Distant Control exercises with the warning word CONTROL. The dog will soon learn what this means.

6 Do enunciate each command very clearly indeed. I have already stressed elsewhere the need to emphasize the vowels in each word of command you use.

In Distant Control it is vital to alter the pitch of your voice very definitely for each command. Use the best bass voice you can muster for DOWN, a mid tone for STAND and preface the command with the dog's name. Use a higher pitch for SIT.

For the purpose of Distant Control some people prefer to use the command BACK rather than STAND when bringing the dog up from either the Down or the Sit. When dealing with the Stand exercise earlier in the book (see p. 70) I stressed the need for training your dog to virtually stand up without moving his feet. This is an excellent basis for Distant Control, but in fact the dog does need a little more room to move than this suggests. So by using the command BACK you are instructing him that this small additional movement must be backwards rather than forwards. The technique I recommended for teaching him to stand was by moving your left hand down his left flank and thence very gently locking back his left leg against the joint. If this is practised regularly it should instil in him the habit of moving his back legs backwards and not forwards. It is the two Stand elements which cause most problems in Distant Control because of the tendency to move forward. The only answer is to teach him the correct movements, with just a two-foot length of cane or batten laid across in front of his forefeet to act as the designated point. If necessary, his movements may be physically restricted by such devices as working him in a corner with some low wire netting stretched across in front of him, or in the angle made by two walls with two chairs laid on their sides to prevent undue movement in the other two directions. Another alternative is the use of three sides of a cardboard carton in the manner shown in pl. 16. To permit the small amount of essential movement, the distance allowed him from front to back should be about twelve inches more than his own body length in the Down position.

In competition the judge usually provides the handler with a card detailing the sequence in which the test is to be performed. The ring steward merely calls out the number against each element for the handler to give the corresponding command to his dog. When practising, it is advisable to hold up a blank card or just your hand in the reading position. This is a further clue to the dog, at the same time obviating any likelihood of his interpreting the raised hand as a signal during competitions. Incidentally some handlers prefer to use hand-signals rather than voice-commands for Distant Control.

To prevent anticipation, change the sequence in which you practise the elements of the exercise frequently and even vary the number of elements each time.

17

Advanced Stand, Sit and Down (ASSD)

The Heel Free Test in both Classes B and C require handler and dog to walk at fast, slow and normal pace as directed by the judge, with ASSD being introduced in Class C. This requires the dog, while walking at Heel at normal pace, to be left at the Stand, Sit and Down positions, in any order, as and when directed by the judge. The handler continues alone as directed by the judge until he reaches his dog, when both must continue together until halted by the judge.

The essence of this exercise is that the dog must assume the position to which he is directed immediately he receives the command and the handler must not hesitate either in leaving the dog, or in the later pick-up. The whole exercise must be one fluid movement.

This is not an exercise which should be taught early in a dog's career, and not at all unless, and until, you desire to enter him in Class C, as it can well ruin his normal heelwork completely. If and when you do start his training it is advisable to give him a command and simultaneously stop by his side and then move off again, rather like a Stay exercise. This will get him used to two things: obeying the command immediately and without forward movement and the fact that you move away leaving him behind. The next stage is merely to hesitate rather than stop when you give a command. When he is reliable you can start to practise the exercise proper and continue without pausing.

When in competition your ASSD commands will be either

vocal or by hand-signal, but not both. While training however, it is essential for vocal commands to be issued in a
clipped and decisive voice and the hand-signals exaggerated.
If the dog hesitates on the DOWN command, push him down
smartly.

18

Dog-training Clubs

As I advised previously, you should join a good dog-training club once you have decided to enter the competitive world. Not only will you learn a great deal, but clubs are also able to keep you advised of forthcoming competitions. In addition, your local paper will probably provide you with venues and dates of the small local shows. Most affiliated clubs, and indeed many of the private ones, subscribe to the magazine *Dog Training Weekly*, the official journal of the Dog-training Clubs of Great Britain, and a number of copies are usually available for scrutiny by members on training nights. This magazine contains full details of forthcoming shows.

Attendance on training nights will give both you and your dog the essential experience of working with the distractions of other dogs and people. Similarly valuable will be the coaching and criticism from (hopefully) experienced instructors and the exchange of ideas and information with other handlers.

One of the many ways in which instructors can help you in training is to act in exactly the same way as the ring steward at shows, by calling out all the instructions to you. This will accustom both you and your dog to reacting in immediate response to orders from a steward. An experienced dog gets to know the orders which his handler is receiving from the steward and in consequence will often anticipate his handler's commands. To obviate this the handler must quite frequently either ignore the instructor's orders, or delay passing on the command to his dog, or even issue a completely different command.

Appendix

Commands used throughout the book

CLEAN DOG	Urinate or defecate where and when you direct.
NO	Stop doing whatever it is you are doing. Note: This is a negative command, so once other commands have been learned, the use of NO should either be dropped whenever possible, or used in conjunction with a positive command (e.g. NO . . . SIT.)
SIT	Sit.
DOWN (or FLAT)	Lie on stomach.
OFF	In the sense of 'get off something' (e.g. the settee).
NAME	Keep it short – preferably single-syllable.
DINNER	Come and get it.
COME	Come here.
BED (or BOX or BASKET)	Go to your bed.
LEAVE	Leave it alone immediately (e.g. another dog or something – probably – undesirable).
IN	Get in (e.g. the car).
OUT	Get out (e.g. the car).
HEEL	Assume the position close to the handler's left leg whether dog is sitting, standing or moving forward.

Commands used throughout the book

BAD (or BAD DOG)	Reasonably severe reprimand.
FREE	You are released temporarily (e.g. from training) or may relax for a moment.
THAT'LL DO	You are released from the session of training or work.
CLOSE	Come in closer to me (e.g. during heelwork or at the Sit).
WATCH ME	Pay attention – concentrate.
WAIT	Remain still just where you are, until I give you another command.
STRAIGHT	e.g. Sit straight (in front of me or in Heel position).
HOLD (or FETCH)	Retrieve it.
GIVE	Give it to me – release it.
STAY	Stay where you are and don't move until I return.
	SIT . . . STAY DOWN . . . STAY } Stays can be in any STAND . . . STAY of these positions.
STAND	Stand up (from Sit or Down).
SPEAK	Bark.
QUIET	Stop barking.
STEADY	Calm down – Slow down – Take it easy.
DROP (or DROP IT)	Spit it out at once.
ROLL OVER	Roll over on your back.
FRONT	Assume the Present position.
BACK	If moving, ease back a bit (e.g. during heelwork). If stationary, move backwards or go back (as opposed to come towards me).
FIND IT	Go and find it (used solely for Hide and Seek).
SCENT BACK	Go back the way we came and use your nose to find an article I have dropped.

117

SEARCH	Look for it (used only for tracking).
SEEK	Go and find it (used only for Scent Discrimination).
CARRY	Carry it for me (e.g. newspaper).
AWAY (or GO)	Go away from me – Straight ahead (used only for the Sendaway).